"Here," he said in that husky voice of his.

He held her by the shoulders and made her stand up straight. "Are you too cold?"

Her face, her hands, her feet—yes. But other parts of her?

CJ pushed the hood back for her. The rush of air around the back of her neck made her shiver. "A little," she said, but anything else she wanted to add died on her tongue when he reached up and began to pull the zipper of her suit down.

He was unwrapping her. Slowly.

Oh, yeah—some parts of her were beginning to burn. She wanted to shift her feet to take some of the pressure off her center, but she didn't want to break the spell of this exact moment.

"You never did tell me the other way of warming someone up." She was surprised to hear her own voice come out deeper—more sultry.

Because she wanted this. Not the story, not her ratings—the man.

* * *

Rich Rancher for Christmas is part of the Beaumont Heirs series—One Colorado family, limitless scandal!

Dear Reader,

Welcome back to Colorado! The Beaumonts Heirs are one of Denver's oldest, most preeminent families. The Beaumont heirs are the children of Hardwick Beaumont. Although he's been dead for almost a decade, Hardwick's womanizing ways—the four marriages and divorces, the ten children and uncounted illegitimate children—are still leaving ripples in the Beaumont family.

Especially now that some of those illegitimate children are revealing themselves. CJ Wesley wasn't happy when his half brothers dragged his parentage into the spotlight. He's a rancher who just wants to be left alone. So far, no one knows his birth father's identity and CJ is going to keep it that way.

But television personality Natalie Baker needs a ratings boost—and an exclusive reveal of another Beaumont bastard's identity is just the ticket. She tracks CJ down with a plan—but she never expects the blizzard that strands her out on his ranch for Christmas. CJ doesn't trust Natalie—but she's not the same woman who smiles at him from his TV. Will Natalie reveal CJ's secret—or will she trust him with her own?

Rich Rancher for Christmas is a sensual story about fighting for your dreams and falling in love. I hope you enjoy reading this book as much as I enjoyed writing it! Be sure to stop by sarahmanderson.com and sign up for my newsletter at eepurl.com/nv39b to join me as I say, Long Live Cowboys!

Sarah

SARAH M. ANDERSON

RICH RANCHER FOR CHRISTMAS

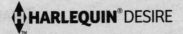

Recycling programs
for this product may
not exist in your area.

ISBN-13: 978-0-373-73502-0

Rich Rancher for Christmas

Printed in U.S.A.

www.Harlequin.com

Sarah M. Anderson may live east of the Mississippi River, but her heart lies out west on the Great Plains. Sarah's book *A Man of Privilege* won an *RT Book Reviews* 2012 Reviewers' Choice Best Book Award. *The Nanny Plan* was a 2016 RITA® Finalist.

Sarah spends her days having conversations with imaginary cowboys and billionaires. Find out more about Sarah's heroes at sarahmanderson.com and sign up for the new-release newsletter at eepurl.com/nv39b.

Books by Sarah M. Anderson

Harlequin Desire

The Nanny Plan
His Forever Family
A Surprise for the Sheikh
Claimed by the Cowboy

The Bolton Brothers

Straddling the Line
Bringing Home the Bachelor
Expecting a Bolton Baby

The Beaumont Heirs

Not the Boss's Baby
Tempted by a Cowboy
A Beaumont Christmas
His Son, Her Secret
Falling for Her Fake Fiancé
His Illegitimate Heir
Rich Rancher for Christmas

Visit her Author Profile page at Harlequin.com, or sarahmanderson.com, for more titles.

To my mom, Carolyn, who insisted I take touch-
typing in high school instead of welding.
You were right. But then, you usually are!

One

An old-fashioned bell chimed as Natalie Baker shoved the door open at Firestone Grain and Feed. Oh, the amount of dirt on that thing—she hoped it hadn't ruined her expensive skirt. Except for the pine boughs and holly that hung in the windows, the entire store looked like it had been rolled through a pasture. She was a long way from downtown Denver.

"Help you?" a man wearing suspenders over a flannel shirt asked from behind the counter. His eyes widened as he took in her five-inch heels and her legs. By the time his gaze had worked its way back up to her perfectly contoured face and professional blow-out, his mouth had flopped open, too.

The only thing missing was a stick of grass hanging out of his lips.

"Hello," Natalie said in her best television voice. "I could use a little help."

"You lost?" He looked her over again and she had to wonder if he'd ever had a woman in heels in this feed store before. God knew she wouldn't be here if there were any other option. "You look lost. I can get you back to Denver. Take a left out of the parking lot and—"

She managed an innocent blush and then looked up at him through her lashes. His eyebrows rose. *Excellent.* He was a malleable kind of man.

"Actually," she began, practically purring, "I'm looking for someone. I was hoping you might know him?"

The old man's chest puffed up with pride. *Perfect.*

She *was* looking for someone—that part was the truth. Her information was that Isabel Santino had married a local rancher by the name of Patrick Wesley in the small ranching town of Firestone, Colorado. It had taken Natalie months to track down the marriage certificate in the county courthouses.

That's how long it had been since the Beaumont bastards had revealed themselves to the public, back in September. Zeb Richards was the oldest of Hardwick Beaumont's illegitimate children. Through a great deal of underhanded dealings that were rumored to be possibly illegal and definitely unethical, he had taken control of the Beaumont Brewery. When Richards had done so, he had had another one of Hardwick's bastard sons, Daniel Lee, standing next to him. The two brothers now ran the brewery and, according to their last quarterly statement, their market share was up eight percent.

But there was more to the story than that. Richards had slipped up at a press conference when Natalie had flashed her very best smile at him and he had admitted that there was a third bastard out there. She hadn't been able to get any more information out of him, but that had been enough.

The Beaumont bastards were big, big news. Natalie's show, *A Good Morning with Natalie Baker*, had been milking the Beaumont family drama for months. It'd been easy, for a while. Zeb Richards had taken over the brewery and then had gotten the brewmaster pregnant. Apparently, he had fallen in love with Casey Johnson—or, at least, they were putting on an exceptionally good public face. They had mostly been seen at the playoffs and the World Series—and at their wedding, of course. That alone had fueled a twelve-percent ratings jump throughout the fall.

But it was December now. Richards and his new wife were old news and would stay that way until she had her baby. That was a good six months off and Natalie's ratings couldn't coast that long.

She had tried to dig into Daniel Lee's past, but

that had proved nearly impossible. It was as if he'd been erased from the public system. No one knew anything about him other than he'd started running political campaigns a few years ago, but even then, she couldn't find anything. He was reputed to play hard and dirty—just like a Beaumont, she figured—but any question Natalie had asked about Lee had been met with a blank stare and a shrug.

That left her with one option and one option only: the mysterious third Beaumont bastard. Which presented its own special set of challenges because no one knew anything about the man except that he existed.

Natalie needed this story because she needed her show. Without it, what did she have?

"Well now, I know just about everyone around these parts. I'm sure I can help you out," the old man said. "Who are you looking for?"

"I believe his name is Carlos Julián Santino? He also might go by Wesley." She batted her eyelashes at the old man. "Do you know where I might be able to find him?"

The old man's grin cracked and he looked significantly less welcoming. "Who?" he asked after a long moment.

That long moment told her things. Specifically, it told her that this feed store owner knew exactly who she was talking about—but he wasn't about to give it away. *Interesting.* She was getting closer.

"His mother's name was Isabel? She might go by Isabella."

"Sorry, missy, but I don't know anyone by those names."

"Are you sure?" She fluttered her eyelashes at him. "I can make it worth your while."

The old man's cheeks shot red. "Can't help you," he grunted, retreating a step. "Do you need any cat food? Dog food? Horse feed? Salt licks?"

Dammit. She was getting closer, she could feel it—but she had overplayed her hand.

An insidious voice whispered in the back of her head—*you can't do this.* Natalie tried to push that voice away, but it was persistent. It always was.

She needed to find Carlos Julián Santino. *A Good Morning* was everything she had and she couldn't let a little something like the lack of exclusive celebrity gossip be the final thing to take her down.

Still, she wasn't going to find out anything else in this feed store. Maybe there was a café or a diner in town. She'd only started here because, as far as she could tell, Patrick Wesley owned a ranch where his family raised beef cattle and surely, cattle ate... something. She wasn't even sure if the Isabel Santino who had married Patrick Wesley was the same Isabel Santino listed on the birth certificate from the Swedish Medical Center in Denver. There was no mention of any child in the marriage certificate and, try as she might, Natalie had been unable to turn up any adoption record between Patrick Wesley and Carlos Julián Santino.

So she could still be wrong. But given the feed store owner's reaction? She didn't think she was.

She slipped one of her business cards out of her coat pocket and forced her most winning smile back onto her face, as if she weren't grossly disappointed. "Well, if you hear anything, why don't you give me a call?" She pushed the card across the counter.

The man did not reach out and pick up the card, so Natalie left it in the dust. She turned to go...only to find herself directly in the sights of a tall, dark and extremely handsome cowboy.

"Oh!" She put a fluttering hand to her chest, playing up her delicate sensibilities to the hilt. "I didn't see you there."

The cowboy's face was in dark shadows under the brim of his black hat, but she could tell he was watching her. Had he been there the entire time? It would be easier to flirt with him if he hadn't seen her flirting with the old man.

Of course, it would be easier to flirt with this cowboy, period. Even though he was wearing a thick sheepskin coat, she could tell his shoulders were broad. He didn't look like a man pretending to be a cowboy—he looked like a man who worked with his hands day in and day out. What kind of muscles were underneath that coat?

"Who are you looking for?" he asked, his voice deep and low and carrying just a hint of menace.

A delicious shiver went through her that had nothing to do with the cold. Her gaze dropped to where his hands rested on his hips. Dear God, look at those hands. Massive and rough-looking—a working man's hands. Not smooth and polished and manicured. Not perfect. But *real*. How would those hands feel on her skin? Her body tensed at the thought of his fingers tracing a line down her chest, circling her nipples…

Oh, she could have a lot of fun with a cowboy like him. If she hadn't had an audience, she might've told him that she was looking for *him*.

But she did have an audience. And a lead to chase. So she put on her most sultry smile. "Have you ever heard of Isabel Santino or Carlos Santino?"

His reaction to these names was so subtle she almost missed it, but a muscle ticked in his jaw. He tilted his head back—not far enough that she could see his eyes, but far enough she knew he was looking her up and down. She rolled her shoulders forward and popped out a hip—her Marilyn Monroe pose. It was usually *very* effective.

Today must not be her day, though. Not even the best that Marilyn had to offer got anything out of this cowboy. He might look like a fantasy come to life, but he clearly wasn't going to play along. "Wilmer's right—I've never heard of either of those people, certainly not here. And this is a small town."

"What about Wesley?"

She saw that muscle in his jaw twitch again. "Pat Wesley? Sure, everybody knows Pat." He tilted his head down again, hiding the rest of his face in shadows. "He's not here, though."

All the smiling was beginning to make her cheeks tight. "Where is he?"

She had couched the question in a sultry tone but the corner of the cowboy's mouth twitched up—was he laughing at her?

He leaned an elbow against a stack of feedbags. He wasn't her type—but there was something so gritty about this cowboy that she couldn't look away. "Why do you want to know? Pat's just a rancher. Keeps to himself—lived here his whole life. Not much to tell, really."

This cowboy was not following the script. He wasn't taking her seriously and he wasn't falling under her spell. Most importantly, he wasn't giving her anything she could use. Quiet ranchers who kept to themselves did not make for good headlines.

"Do you know if he has an adopted son?" She knew that Carlos Julián Santino would be thirty-four years old. She didn't know how old this cowboy was—there was no way to tell, with his face in the shadows like it was.

There was that twitching in his jaw again. But he said, "Ma'am, I assure you he does not."

What if she were wrong? *Of course you're wrong*, the voice in the back of her head scolded her.

It was ridiculous for her to have thought she could find the one man nobody else could. *She* was ridiculous, pinning all her hopes and dreams for ratings gold, for fame and fortune, onto the Beaumonts and their various and sundry bastards.

She swallowed down the bitter disappointment. Unexpectedly, the cowboy tilted his head to one side, letting a little light spill across his features. It was a damn shame he wasn't more helpful—or more interested—because he was simply gorgeous. He had a strong jaw with a healthy two-week stubble coming in that made her want to stroke his face and other things. What color were his eyes?

No, she shouldn't be thinking about this guy's eyes. She should be focused on her end goal—finding the lost Beaumont bastard. What would his eyes be like? Dark? Or light? Zeb Richards's eyes were a bright green—which really stood out on a black man. She didn't know if Carlos Santino's eyes would be light or dark.

Still, she wanted to see what this cowboy's eyes looked like. Would they tell her something that his body wasn't? If she could get a good look at his eyes, would she see wariness—or want?

He tilted his head back down, throwing his face

completely in shadows again. *Crap.* This was not her lucky day. This man was immune to her charms and she couldn't stand in a feed store all day. She might not be very smart, but even she knew when to cut her losses. She pulled out another card and offered it to the cowboy. "If you find out anything, I can make it worth your while."

He didn't take the card. "I'm sure you can, Ms. Baker." He stepped toward her and Natalie tensed. He knew who she was? Was he a viewer? A fan? Or was he one of those anonymous internet trolls who made her skin crawl even as she craved their attention?

Because when they were insulting her, at least they were paying attention. She was *someone*, even if she was someone they despised.

But he stepped around her, careful to cut a wide enough berth that there was no accidental touching. Instead, he went to the counter and leaned against it, his entire body angled toward Wilmer.

The body language was clear. It was them against her.

She did what she always did when she felt insecure—she took up as much space as she could. She straightened her shoulders and shot another one of her best smiles at the two men.

She said, "Gentlemen," even though it was pretty clear that was a loosely applied term at best. And then, head held high, she walked out of the Firestone Grain and Feed and contemplated her next move.

"What the heck was that all about?" Wilmer asked, scratching the back of his head.

CJ Wesley kept an eye on the woman through the grimy windows of the feed store. She stood on the front step, no doubt plotting where to look for him next. Jesus, Natalie Baker was even more gorgeous in real life than she was on television. And in that outfit?

He knew what she was wearing was part of her act. No sane human would drive out to the windswept northern hills of Colorado in December in a skin-tight black skirt that, with black lace overlaying a black silk lining, looked exactly as warm as a bathing suit. Between the skirt and the sky-high heels—he was damn impressed at how she walked in them—her legs were what men wrote poetry about.

CJ cleared his throat. He wasn't a poet and he wasn't interested in Natalie Baker. As he watched, she stepped carefully down the stairs and moved toward a red convertible—a Mustang. Was there any car less appropriate for December in Colorado than that one?

Then again, everything about Natalie Baker was inappropriate, from her amazing cleavage to her fake smiles to her terrifying questions.

"No idea," CJ lied.

"She's one of those TV people," Wilmer said, and CJ had to wonder if Wilmer had just figured that out. He was many things, but Wilmer was not a morning-chat-show guy. If anyone paid even the slightest attention to the morning shows, they'd recognize Natalie Baker immediately. She kept her finger firmly on the pulse of the Denver social scene. If a sports star cheated on his wife, an actress fell in love or, say, a billionaire fathered a bunch of illegitimate children, Natalie Baker was there.

Which meant she was *here*.

Of course, CJ knew Natalie Baker was a beautiful woman. Her face smiled out at him in high definition every morning. But in real life, she'd not only been more beautiful, but also more…delicate, too. Although that could have just been the juxtaposition of her expensive clothes and perfect makeup with the grime of the feed store.

Wilmer waited until her car was out of sight before speaking again. "What do TV people want with your dad?"

"Don't have a clue," CJ lied again. Because he knew. He knew exactly why Natalie Baker was here. It had very little to do with his father, Patrick Wesley.

It had everything to do with Hardwick Beaumont.

CJ shook his head, hoping Wilmer would read it as confusion. "Dad's not even here," he reminded Wilmer because CJ knew one thing: all the gossip in this town ran through Wilmer. The Firestone Diner was almost as bad, but Wilmer Higgins at the Firestone Grain and Feed was officially worse. CJ had to get out in front of this and make sure Wilmer had his version of events before anyone started looking around too hard. "You know that man's never done a scandalous thing in his life."

It helped that Pat Wesley had lived in Firestone for all of his fifty-six years. Everyone thought they knew everything about him and not a damn bit of it was scandalous. He was the third generation of Wesleys to raise beef cattle on his land—CJ was the fourth. As far as this town was concerned, the most outrageous thing Patrick Wesley had ever done was marry a woman named Bell that he'd met while he was in the army instead of the girl who'd been his high-school sweetheart. But that had been thirty-three years ago, and since then?

CJ knew exactly how dull his dad was. It was not a bad thing. Patrick Wesley was a good man and a good father, but his idea of a wild Friday night was driving to the next town over to eat at Cracker Barrel and even then, he'd be home by eight and snoring in his recliner by eight thirty. Safe? Yes. Reliable? Absolutely.

Newsworthy? Not a shot in hell.

CJ didn't know what made him madder about the sudden appearance of the gorgeous Natalie Baker asking questions—that the people he'd grown up with might one day figure out he wasn't actually

Pat's son or that, once they found out, they might treat Pat and Bell Wesley differently.

He knew who Natalie was, of course. She was hard to miss. Her beautiful face was on his screen every morning at seven thirty. CJ didn't actually like her show—it was too much gossip and innuendo about celebrities. But she also seemed to be the first to know anything about the Beaumonts. It wasn't like CJ religiously followed them. Hell, he didn't even like their beer. But he liked to stay informed. And that meant he caught *A Good Morning with Natalie Baker* most days.

Besides, it wasn't like he was watching it for her. He wasn't. Yes, she was beautiful on screen and, okay, she was stunning in real life. That had nothing to do with anything. He preferred that station's morning weatherman to the other options, that was all. So watching her show was just a matter of convenience, really.

"I know," Wilmer said, snapping his suspenders. "It just don't make a lick of sense. I mean, you weren't adopted."

CJ forced himself to smile. "That's what they tell me," he said in a joking tone. It was a relief when Wilmer chuckled. "Clearly, they have the wrong Wesley." Wilmer nodded and CJ took advantage of the pause to ask about the latest supplements for his horses. Wilmer enjoyed gossip, but he wasn't about to miss out on a chance to sell a feed supplement.

CJ didn't actually want the supplement but it was a small price to pay for distracting Wilmer from one Ms. Natalie Baker. He finished up his regular order with a sample of the new supplement and headed out to his truck.

He was going to have to tell his mother. She had lived in fear of the day when the Beaumonts would come for him. He had heard all the stories and, for years now, had followed all the headlines. He knew Hardwick Beaumont was dead and the idea didn't bother him even a little. He couldn't even bring himself to think of the man as his father—not even his birth father. Hardwick had been nothing more than a sperm donor. Patrick Wesley was his father in every sense of the word. He knew it, his parents knew it and the state of Colorado knew it. End of discussion.

God, this was going to upset his mother. She had relaxed after Hardwick's death—although by then, CJ had been twenty-one and a man in his own right. But Bell Wesley had lived in fear that Hardwick Beaumont would come for her son for so long that worrying about it was a reflexive habit she couldn't break. It was one of the reasons why his parents wintered in Arizona now. The Denver TV stations were saturated with Beaumont Brewery Christmas commercials this time of year and it always upset her. And his dad hated it when his mom was upset.

CJ always missed them at Christmas, but otherwise, he was glad to have the place to himself. And when they came back from wintering in Arizona, they were happy and relaxed and everything went smoothly.

This year, he was even gladder they were in Arizona. If Natalie Baker had found his mother and started asking questions, Mom might've had a nervous breakdown.

He drove slowly through town, keeping his eyes peeled. It was impossible to miss her Mustang parked in front of the diner.

Damn it all. He knew deep in his heart that he had not seen the last of that woman. Isabel might've gone by Bell and they might've downplayed her being Hispanic, but it was a damn short leap from Carlos Julián to CJ.

It was only a matter of time until he was outed as one of the Beaumont bastards.

Two

There were many things Natalie wasn't—talented, pretty, likable, smart—but no one could say she wasn't persistent. Even her father would have to grudgingly admit that she didn't give up when the going got tough. It was maybe the only valuable lesson he'd ever taught her.

She shivered in her car, cranking the heat up a little more—not that it made a difference. The winds were blowing out of what she assumed was the north with a howling ferocity and there was no way her trusty Mustang was going to keep the chill at bay.

She'd spent the better part of the last three weeks visiting Firestone, making friends with the locals and trying to weasel out more information about

Patrick Wesley and his family. It had not been easy. For starters, the coffee at the diner was awful and no one in this town had ever heard of a latte. More than that, it felt like the town had closed ranks. Just like that handsome cowboy and the feed store owner had.

Natalie was an outsider and they weren't going to allow her in.

Still, she had just enough celebrity cachet to razzle-dazzle some of the locals. She was famous enough and pretty enough and she knew how to use those assets like laser-guided weapons. She had spent weeks flirting and smiling and cooing and touching the shoulders of men who probably knew better but were flattered by a young woman paying attention to them.

Maybe they did know better. Because it hadn't been one of the old geezers who'd finally slipped up. It had been a younger man, in his late twenties and full of swagger. He'd been the only real threat to her. The old guys never would've followed up on her flirtations, which was why it was safe to make them. But this guy had seen her as someone he could use just as much as she could use him.

He had finally given her what she wanted, after she had made some vague promises that maybe the next time he was in Denver, he should look her up. It turned out that Pat Wesley—who appeared to be some sort of saint, according to the locals—*did* have a son. That in and of itself wasn't so unusual.

But his son's name was CJ.

Carlos Julián Santino *had* to be CJ Wesley. There was simply no other alternative.

She rubbed her arms over her coat, trying to keep the blood circulating through some of her body. She had been sitting outside of the house on Wesley land for half an hour and she wasn't sure how much longer she could take it. It was *freezing*.

She kept going over the questions she'd ask this Wesley guy. Maybe it was the mind-numbing cold, though, because her thoughts kept drifting back to the second person she'd talked to—the tall, dark cowboy in the feed store.

Despite the amount of time she'd spent in Firestone over the last three weeks, she hadn't seen him again. Not that she'd been looking—she hadn't. He'd made his position clear. He would not help her and she couldn't afford to waste time on a dead end.

But that hadn't stopped her from thinking of him. It was hard not to—not when she peeled that heavy sheepskin coat off his body and threw his hat to the side in her dreams. She'd spent weeks waking up frustrated and achy, all because of one cowboy with an attitude problem.

What had his eyes looked like? Did he watch her show? Did he ever wonder what she was like?

While she mused, she kept scrolling through Twitter. Her last tweet—a tease about tomorrow's big reveal of a "major star" on *A Good Morning*—had only gotten four retweets. She clicked over to Instagram and saw that the cross post had gotten no replies.

Tightness took hold of her chest that had nothing to do with the cold. It'd been like this for weeks now—her reach falling, her interactions dropping off a cliff. If no one paid attention to her, she wouldn't matter. At least if they were mad at her, they were paying attention. But once the attention stopped…

Her phone pinged—a text from her producer, Steve. Anything yet?

Natalie forced herself to breathe once, and then twice. Working on it, she texted back.

The latest numbers are in—you're falling behind. If you can't pull this out, I'm giving your slot to Kevin.

The tightness in her chest squeezed so hard she had trouble breathing. There was no way she could wait until the next Beaumont baby was born—she needed Carlos Julián Santino or CJ Wesley or whatever name he went by and she needed him *now*. She could not lose her spot to Kevin Durante. Kevin had great hair and that was it. He was dumber than a post, lousy in bed and, unfortunately, was exactly the sort of benign golden boy that did well on morning television. She'd rather cut off her toe than give her spot to Kevin.

No worries! she texted back. I'll be in touch.

There was an agonizingly long pause before Steve replied. You better be right about this, Baker.

I won't let you down! she texted back, hoping that sounded far more confident than she felt.

Steve was running out of patience with her. If she lost ground to *Denver This Morning*, then she'd be out of a job, out of broadcasting, out of the public eye. Steve's job security rested entirely on beating *Denver This Morning* in the ratings. She knew damn good and well he wouldn't go down with her ship. He would replace her in a heartbeat if it came to that. With Kevin.

So, she continued to sit in the freezing cold outside of the Wesley house, waiting. The house was dark and she had knocked on every visible door when she'd arrived. She was as confident as she could be without breaking and entering that no one was home.

Okay, she bargained with herself, she would tough it out for ten minutes and if no one showed up she would head back to the diner. The coffee might be god-awful, but it was hot. And maybe that grumpy cowboy would show up.

She spent the next ten minutes toggling between Twitter, Instagram and Facebook, trying to fight the growing sense of panic at the lack of likes and hearts and favorites and retweets. Clearly, her last posts hadn't been shocking enough. Feeling desperate, she posted: Rumor has it that Matthew Beaumont and his child-star bride Whitney Wildz are expecting— but is the baby really his?

She felt a pang of guilt at the lie before she reminded herself that the Beaumonts were a public entity and this was how the game was played. Besides, if anyone could handle the heat, it was PR genius Matthew Beaumont. Really, the Beaumonts should be thanking her. She helped them sell beer, after all.

The guilt successfully contained, she posted and cross-posted the rumor. As the comments added up and the retweets accumulated, the tightness in her chest loosened. This was better. She had a therapist once tell her that her need for approval was unhealthy and she should accept herself for who she was. Natalie had accepted that she was not going back to that therapist ever again.

Still, she was freezing. She put down her phone and went to put her car into Reverse when she saw it—a vaguely familiar pickup truck rolling up behind her. *Oh, thank God*—she was in no mood to die of frostbite out in the middle of nowhere.

Well, well, *well*. If it wasn't a particularly familiar-looking tall, dark, handsome cowboy climbing out of that pickup truck. She should've known. The cowboy in the black hat from the feed store was none other than Carlos Julián Santino Beaumont Wesley. That muscle twitch in his jaw—that was his tell. She had been so close to the truth—why hadn't she seen it?

Her heart did a funny little skip at the sight of him and honestly, she wasn't sure if that was because he was the man she'd been searching for to secure her job for the foreseeable future or…

Or if she was just glad to see him.

That was ridiculous. She wasn't glad to see him and he sure as hell wasn't glad to see her—even at this distance, his scowl was ferocious. She waited until he had shut the door of his truck before she opened her own door. She unfolded her legs slowly, letting her skirt ride up a little so he could catch a glimpse of her thigh as she stood. "We meet again."

A whole lot more than his jaw was twitching. "What the hell are you doing here?"

He was pissed, but she refused to cower. "I believe I've been looking for you, Mr. Santino. Or should I say, Mr. Beaumont?"

She was pushing her luck and she knew it. He was practically vibrating with rage and no amount of bare leg was going to appease him. If only she'd guessed that the man she was looking for was the cowboy from the feed store, she would've at least put on long pants because that cowboy had not been interested in her body. And, by all accounts, he still wasn't.

"My name is Wesley," he said through gritted teeth.

"Sure, we can play it that way. CJ Wesley, right?" With shivering fingers, she pulled out her phone and opened up the camera app.

The next thing she knew, she was staring at her empty hand. She blinked and looked up just in time to see Wesley pocketing her phone. "Hey! Give that back!"

"No," he said, and almost smiled. "I don't think I'm going to. You're on private property, Ms. Baker. You're about two steps away from flat-out stalking me. You've been working your way through the population of Firestone for the last three weeks trying to get out here. I'm trying to think of a good reason why I shouldn't call Jim Bob and have you arrested for stalking, trespassing, and—" His gaze swept over her body. "And sheer stupidity. Did you even look at the weather before you drove out here today? Don't you know there's supposed to be a blizzard that hits tonight? And you're out here in what—a pair of heels and a skirt? You're lucky you're not dead of exposure already."

She stared at him and, for a moment, forgot to arrange herself in the most seductive way possible. The first part of what he said—the trespassing and stalking—wasn't so surprising. She'd had people angry at her before.

But the part about the blizzard and exposure? He was mad at her—perhaps justifiably—but it had almost sounded like he was concerned about her. "Our meteorologist said it wasn't going to hit until tomorrow."

"Get in your car," he said sharply.

The force of his words backed her up a bit. Although it could have been the wind. "What? No! You're crazy if you think I'm going anywhere without my phone."

Unexpectedly, he jerked his head up and looked at the sky. Dark, she realized. His eyes were a deeper color—hazel? Maybe light brown. Not the light green of so many of the Beaumonts. The shadow from the brim of his hat had to have been the reason why she hadn't seen the Beaumont in his face in the feed store. Every Beaumont man had the same jawline. CJ Wesley was no exception.

She was beginning to shake, the wind was that vicious. She eyed his heavy sheepskin coat with jealousy. "Look," she began, "I'm sure there's something—"

"Ms. Baker," he interrupted, "get in your car and start driving. That storm isn't going to hit tomorrow. It's coming. Now." As he spoke, he reached back into the bed of his truck and pulled out several grocery bags. "And I'm not giving you your phone back. I'll take a hatchet to it before I let you take pictures of me and splash them all over God's green earth. My life is not for sale." He looked up at the sky and grimaced. "City slickers," he mumbled, she thought.

He brushed past her, moving too fast for her to grab him and get her phone out of his pocket. He set down the groceries on the porch and fumbled with his keys.

She just stood there, gaping at him. "I am *not* leaving without my phone." Her life was on that phone—her connection to the world. If she didn't have it…well, she didn't have anything.

He stopped as he got the door open and turned back to her. "You leave right now or you won't be leaving at all." He pointed at the sky behind her.

Reluctantly, Natalie turned her face into the wind. It was so bitingly strong that it was hard to keep her eyes open. Finally, she saw what he was talking about. It wasn't just the gray sky that had washed the colors out of the landscape—it was a huge gray cloud. Suddenly, she could tell that it was moving—quickly. The cloud was bearing down on them, erasing the landscape underneath it. It was a living, moving thing—a wall of swirling white. She hadn't noticed because she'd been too busy looking at her phone and then at him. There weren't many buildings around here to use as landmarks, but it was clear now that the storm was almost upon her and that she was *screwed*.

For the first time that day, she felt real fear. Not just the everyday anxiety that she struggled with all the time—no, this was a true, burning fear. Storms in Denver could be a weather event—but there were snowplows and twenty-four-hour pharmacies. There were snow shovels and sidewalks, and sooner rather than later, she would be able to get out and move around her city.

But now she was in the middle of nowhere with a blizzard about to hit. This wasn't the makings of a white Christmas. And given that she was already half-frozen, it wouldn't take much to finish her off.

She didn't know how long she stood there, staring at the cloud wall. Time seemed to slow down the faster the storm moved. Then, suddenly, she was in the wall of snow and wind. She tried to scream, but the wind tore her cries out of her throat and threw them away. Her first instinct was to curl into a ball and shield her nearly bare legs, but dimly, in the back of her mind, she knew she needed to move. Standing still meant death. Not the slow death of a ratings slide. A real, irreversible, not-coming-back-from-it death.

She stumbled to one side, but the wind pushed her back. Her car! She looked around but couldn't even see the Mustang. There was nothing but gray and stinging snowflakes and blisteringly cold wind.

Then, unexpectedly, she felt something warm and solid at her back. Arms closed around her waist and physically lifted her into the air. *Wesley*. Her first instinct was to struggle—but the fact that he was warm overrode everything else. She let him carry her, trusting that he knew where he was and where he was going. After what seemed like an hour but was probably only a minute or two, a dark shape loomed out of the snow—the house. He carried her up steps and thrust her through the door, where she promptly tripped over the groceries. She landed with a thud on her bottom, dazed and freezing and wet.

She looked up and saw Wesley struggling to get the door shut. He put his shoulder into it and slammed it against the wind, and instantly, she felt at least ten degrees warmer.

"Thank you," she said. Well, she tried to say it. Her teeth were chattering so hard what came out sounded more like a keyboard clicking.

Wesley loomed over her, his hands on his hips. At some point, he'd lost his hat, which meant that for the first time, she had a really good look at his face. His hair was a deep brown and his face was tanned. He had snowflakes stuck to his two-week beard. She couldn't stop shivering, but he just stood there like an immovable boulder.

An *angry* immovable boulder.

She didn't like the way he was looking at her, as if he could see exactly how worthless she felt. So, still shaking so hard that she could barely get her feet under her, she stood. It was then she realized she'd lost one of her shoes. Dammit, those had been Dolce & Gabbana.

"Thank you," she said again. It came out less clicky this time. "I'll just warm up and then I'll go." She swallowed. "I'd like my phone back, please, but I promise I won't take any pictures of you." It hurt to make that promise because her producer was expecting results and without them…

CJ Wesley had just saved her life. He obviously didn't like her, but he'd still dragged her into his house. And for that, she was grateful.

"You don't get it, do you?"

She could be grateful and still be irritated at the tone in his voice, right? "Get what?"

"The convertible of yours? It's not four-wheel drive, is it?"

"No…"

He sighed heavily and looked toward the ceiling. "I send you back out in this, assuming you can even get to your car before you freeze to death in that getup," he said, waving a dismissive hand at her outfit, "you won't make it off the property. You'll drive off the road, get stuck in a ditch and freeze to death before nightfall." He leveled a hard gaze at her and all of her self-defense mechanisms failed her. She shrank back. "You're stuck here, Ms. Baker. You're stuck here with me for the duration."

Three

"What?"

CJ had to stop himself from stepping forward and brushing the snowflakes from her eyelashes. She was an ice princess right now, the White Witch of Winter. If he wasn't careful, she just might bewitch him. "You're not going anywhere."

She shuddered again and this time, he didn't think it was entirely from the cold. Now what? Maybe he should have just left her out there, since he couldn't seem to get rid of her any other way.

But even as he thought it, he felt guilty. That was not the Wesley way and he knew it. So now, it appeared he would be spending the next several days—possibly even Christmas—with Natalie Baker. The one woman who had not only figured out he was related to Hardwick Beaumont, but also wanted to use that knowledge for…for what? Ratings?

"I could…" She looked out the front window. CJ looked with her. It was a solid mass of gray. It could've been fog, except for the small particles of snow and ice pinging off the window.

"No, you can't. I'm not going to let you freeze to death out there." He gritted his teeth. How was he going to keep her out of his business if she were physically stuck in his house?

How was he going to keep his hands off of her if she were stuck in his house?

Hell, he'd already failed at that. He'd picked her up and all but slung her over his shoulder like he was a caveman, dragging her back to his cave. Her body had been cold, yes—but also soft and light and…

"You're probably freezing," he went on, trying to stay in the present.

Because the present was a wet woman who was criminally underdressed. He needed to get her warmed up before she caught her death. And given the way the wind was howling out there, he didn't have a lot of time. "You better take a hot shower while we still have power. And if there's anyone you need to call to let them know you're all right, you should do that now." She opened her mouth but he cut her off. "You can use my house phone."

He wanted her to move, or at least do something—

but she didn't. Instead she looked at him with a mixture of confusion and anxiety. "Are you being nice to me?"

"No," he answered quickly, even though it was a lie and they both knew it. "But I don't want your death on my hands."

That statement sobered her up. "Oh."

She sounded small and vulnerable and dammit, that pulled at something inside of him. But he wasn't going to listen to that something because he liked to think he wasn't an idiot. And only an idiot would fall for whatever Natalie Baker was trying to pull over him. She'd spent weeks hunting for him and she'd already tried to use her fabulous body as an enticement on more than one occasion. For all he knew, she had decided raw sexuality wouldn't work and instead was making a play for his heartstrings.

It wasn't going to work. He was immune to all the vulnerability she was projecting right now. "Who do you need to call?"

He wouldn't have thought it possible, but she seemed to get even smaller. "Well, I guess…" There was a long pause. "Well…" she said again, blinking furiously. "No one."

He stared at her. "You're probably going to be here for Christmas, you realize that, right?" Surely, there had to be someone who would miss her. She was a famous TV personality. He'd recognized her the moment she set foot in the feed store. Someone as beautiful and talented as Natalie Baker... Even if she didn't have close family, she had to have friends.

She shook her head. Then she tried to smile. "I'm not going to lie, the shower sounds great. I don't think I've ever been this cold."

He eyed her clothes again. She kicked out of her other shoe, and suddenly, she barely came up to his shoulder. She had nothing on her legs but a tight, short skirt underneath a peacoat in a wild fuchsia color. He couldn't decide if she was oblivious or just stupid about the weather. Or if she'd planned it this way—planned on getting herself trapped out here with him.

Either way, he was willing to get her some dry clothes. That skirt wasn't going to keep her warm even if he got his fireplace cranked up. "All right. But," he said before she could make a move deeper into his house, "these are the rules. I hold on to your phone for as long as you're here and you stay out of my life. Otherwise, it's a hell of a long walk to town in this weather."

He wouldn't really kick her out—but she didn't need to know that.

For a second, a sign of toughness flashed over her face and he thought she was going to argue. But just then, the wind rattled the door and the color— what little of it she'd managed to regain—drained from her face. She nodded, looking almost innocent.

"Understood. I'm sorry that I'm intruding upon your Christmas."

He rolled his eyes. "Are you?"

It wasn't a nice thing to say—thereby proving her wrong. He wasn't being all that nice to her. Which bothered him, even though it shouldn't. It especially bothered him when she had the nerve to look so… defeated. Sure, maybe that was the wet clothes and the straggly hair—and the mascara that had started to slide. The woman before him right now was anything but polished.

Before his guilt could get the better of him, he said, "This way."

This was a mistake because someone like Natalie Baker—he didn't even know what to call her. A journalist? A reporter? A talking head? Well, whatever she was, he knew that he wouldn't be able to keep her out of his life, not if they were going to be stranded here for four or five days. Sooner or later, she'd stumble upon something he didn't want her to see. His baby book or the awkward photo from eighth grade when he accidentally cut his hair into a mullet while trying to be fashionable.

He hoped she'd take a *long* shower so he could do a sweep of the house and hide as much of his life as he could.

He passed the thermostat and cranked it up. It might get warm in the house, but with the way that wind was blowing, they would lose power sooner rather than later. If he hadn't been busy arguing with her, he could've gotten the generator going already. As it was, he'd have to wait until the snow stopped. And who knew when that would be.

Besides, when he glanced back at her, she had her arms wrapped around herself as she trailed after him. Her lips were blue—actually, all of her looked blue. *Crap*. He really did need to get her warmed up.

He led her back to the guest room, which had the advantage of being the room with the least amount of family pictures. As long as they had power, he'd leave her in this room. If he could, he'd lock her in it—but he knew that would only make matters worse. He could see the headline now—Long-Lost Beaumont Bastard Locks Beloved Celebrity in Guest Room.

No, thank you.

The guest room had an attached bathroom. "We're probably going to lose power in the next half hour, so plan accordingly." He thought she nodded—it was hard to tell, because she was shaking so hard.

God, what a mess. He went into the bathroom and turned on the hot water. "Make sure you stay in there until you've returned to a normal temperature."

The other alternative to get her body temperature back up was to strip them both down and crawl under the covers with her.

He looked at her legs again. Long and, when not

borderline frostbitten, probably tanned. The kind of legs that would wrap around him and—

Whoa.

He slammed the brakes on that line of thought something quick. There would be no nudity, no cuddling and absolutely *no* sex. What he had to do right now, as steam curled out of the bathroom and she shrugged out of her fuchsia coat to reveal a thin silk blouse that was soaked at the cuffs and collar, was remember that every single thing he said and did from this point on was as good as public. He wouldn't touch her and, what's more, he wouldn't allow her to touch him. End of discussion.

"I'll bring in some better clothes for you," he said as he headed out of the room. Because if he had a look at her walking around in that tight skirt and that sheer blouse for the next three or four days…

He was a strong man. But even he wasn't sure he was *that* strong. Not if she was going to look all soft and vulnerable as well as sexy.

"Thank you," she said again in that delicate voice.

No, he wasn't going to think of her as vulnerable. Or delicate. It was probably just an act designed to get him to open up to her.

He hurried to his parents' room and dug out some appropriate clothing—long underwear, jeans, shirts and sweaters and socks. His mom was a little shorter and a lot curvier than Natalie Baker, but her things should fit. Better than anything of his, anyway. She'd swim in one of his sweaters.

He knocked on the guest room door and, when no one replied, he cracked it open. Good. The bathroom door was closed and he heard splashing. She was in the shower, then. Standing nude under the hot water, maybe even running the soap over her body, her bare breasts, her...

He hoped she'd locked that damn door. He laid the clothes out on the bed and almost scooped up her things to take them down to the laundry room to dry. But then he caught sight of the lacy bra and matching panties—pale pink, like a confection that she'd worn on her body—and he drew back his hand as if he'd been burned. Okay, so now he was going to *not* think about her body wearing those things. And he also had to *not* think about her *not* wearing those things.

Oh, God. This was a disaster in the making.

He forced his thoughts away from the woman steaming up the shower. He had practical things that he needed to get done. It was obvious she had no idea how to ride out a blizzard, which meant it was up to him to keep them both from freezing to death.

He made sure that every other door on the second floor was shut, then he hurried downstairs, pausing to snag the family photos off the wall. He shoved those into the coat closet. Luckily, he'd laid a fire in the fireplace before he'd gone to town this morning, so all he had to do was light it. Once it was going, he went to the kitchen. He had a roast in a slow cooker, but he turned on the gas oven anyway, just to build up the heat in the house. Once the power went, the wind would sap any warmth from this room in a matter of minutes. And if he just left it on, he wouldn't have to worry about lighting it with a match later.

He scrubbed a couple of potatoes and put them in the oven and then, after a moment of internal debate, dug an apple pie out of the freezer and put it in the oven, too.

Every fall, his mom went into a frenzy of cooking and baking. CJ had long ago figured out that it was her way of coping with the guilt of leaving her only son alone during the holidays. He had an entire deep freeze full of casseroles and cobblers and meals in bags that all he had to do was heat up in the oven or the slow cooker. Pretty much the only thing she didn't leave him was pizza and beer, which was why he'd headed to the store this morning after sending his hired hands home for the storm and cutting his chores short. If he was going to be snowed in for Christmas, he wanted a couple of pizzas to round out the menu.

Then he did another sweep of the downstairs. He pulled more photos from the wall and the mantel over the fireplace. These he carried back to the office—that had a door he could lock. If he could, he'd put the entire house in that room and bolt the door shut.

The parlor was where most of the photo albums were—it had a door, but not a lock. Well, he'd just have to keep her out of it. Much as he didn't like it, he would have to stick to Natalie Baker like glue.

Finally, with dinner underway and as much of his life hidden as he could hide, he headed back up the stairs. Just as he reached the top, she opened her door and stepped out into the hall.

CJ's breath caught in his throat. Gone was the too-polished, too-perfect celebrity. And in her place...

She'd pulled her hair into a low tail at the side. Her face was free of makeup, but somehow she looked even prettier. Softer, definitely.

That softness was dangerous. So was any question he was asking himself right now about whether or not she'd put the lacy pink panties back on.

So he did his best to focus on anything but that. "Better?" he asked in a gruff voice, but he didn't need to ask because he could tell. The color had come back into her cheeks—a natural blush instead of an artfully applied one. Her hair was fair—more blond than it looked on-screen. Without the heavy layer of eye makeup, her eyes seemed wider, more crystal blue.

Bad. This was *bad*.

"Yes, thank you." Even her voice sounded different now. True, she was no longer shivering with cold, but when she was on television, talking to the camera and interviewing stars, her voice had a certain cadence to it, low and husky. That was gone now.

CJ realized with a start that he might be looking at the real Natalie Baker. And he couldn't do that. If he started thinking of her as a real person instead of a talking head, then he might get lost in those blue eyes.

Luckily, the storm saved him from himself. With a pop, all the lights went out. Natalie didn't scream, but he heard her gasp in alarm.

"It's all right," he said, coming the rest of the way to get her. The hall was darker than normal because he'd shut the doors. "It's okay. I'm right here." He reached out to touch her—just to give her a reassuring pat on the shoulder. But when he did so, she latched onto his forearm with a tight, fearful grip.

He sucked in air and fought the sudden urge to wrap his arms around her and keep her safe. Dammit, she was getting to him.

"Sorry," she said, loosening her grip—but not letting him go. "I guess I'm a little jumpy. I'm not normally this poorly prepared."

CJ didn't think he could believe she'd gotten stranded by accident. But whether or not her presence here had been planned didn't change things, at least not for the next few days.

Suddenly, he was aware that they were standing in a mostly dark hallway, touching. He withdrew his hand. "We should grab the pillows and things."

She jerked her head up in surprise. "What?"

"I've got a fire going downstairs in the living room. Once the snow stops, I'll go outside and get the generator started, but until then we should stay in front of the fire." He didn't tell her that he had a fireplace in his room and that there was another one in his parents' room. This wasn't his first blizzard.

He wasn't letting her sleep in his parents' bed— or his. Absolutely no sharing of beds.

He felt her exhale, the warmth of her breath around him. Almost without being aware of it, he started to lean toward her. "Is that so you can keep an eye on me?"

There wasn't any point in lying. Besides, lying did not come naturally to him. Perhaps Hardwick Beaumont had been good at it, but Patrick Wesley was honest to a fault. The only thing he had ever lied about was CJ's mother and CJ. In fact, CJ was sure that Pat had told the lie so many times about marrying Bell on leave and having CJ arrive before he'd been honorably discharged that both his parents believed it, heart and soul.

CJ wanted to believe it, too—because Pat *was* his father. CJ resented the fact that the ghost of Hardwick Beaumont hung over him—always had, always would.

And he resented this woman for bringing Hardwick Beaumont's ghost with her. Yes, the anger felt good. He was going to hold on to that anger for as long as he could. She might be prettier in real life, and that softness about her might call to him, but he was furious at her and that was *that*.

He walked back into the guest room and stripped the blankets and pillows off the bed. "Here," he said, shoving them at her. Then he went to his own room and did the same. There. Now they didn't have a reason to come back upstairs for the next several days.

Wordlessly, he led the way back downstairs to the living room. The fire had taken and the room was bathed in a warm, crackling glow.

He dropped his bedding on the couch and went to work rearranging the room. The coffee table went to the far side under the windows, where it would be darkest and coldest. He pulled the couch forward so it faced the fire and then dragged the recliners over so they boxed in the heat on each side. He laid a blanket over the coffee table so that drafts wouldn't come in underneath it. And then he made a pallet on the floor. "You can take the couch."

Her eyes widened and CJ knew she understood him perfectly. He would sleep on the floor, directly in front of her, to keep her from sneaking off in the night and snooping.

She hesitated. "You've done this before."

He wasn't sure how he was going to talk to her without revealing things. Well, the trick was to reveal as little as possible. "I have. This is not my first blizzard. But I'm gathering that it's your first time."

The moment the words left his mouth, he winced. That was an unfortunate double entendre.

But, gracefully, she ignored his poor choice of words. She fluffed her pillows and shot him a sheepish grin. "I suppose that was obvious. It's different in Denver." She folded her blankets, making a sort of sleeping bag on top of the couch. Then she straightened, her hands on her hips. He got the feeling she was judging her work—and finding it lacking. "I didn't plan this," she said softly. "I'm not... I'm not always a good person. But I want you to know that I didn't come out here with the intent of making you rescue me." She didn't look at him as she said this. Instead, she kept her head down.

If that were the truth—and that was a big *if*—he wondered how much the admission cost her. "Might as well make the best of it. I prefer not to spend the next few days being miserable. It's the Christmas season—good will toward all men *and* women."

She glanced at him, but quickly dropped her eyes again. Her mouth curved down in a way that CJ recognized—it was the kind of smile his mother made when she was trying not to cry.

He didn't want Natalie Baker to cry. She hadn't cried when she'd been half-frozen. Why would she do so now? Finally, after several painful seconds, she whispered, "Peace on earth?"

That was the truce. "Can't promise you a silent night, though—that wind's not going to stop." Her smile was more real this time and somehow it made him feel better. What was wrong with him? It was enough that he had saved her from freezing to death. It was not his responsibility to make her happy. End of discussion.

However, that didn't stop him from adding "Dinner should be ready. We can fill our plates and sit in front of the fire."

She followed him into the kitchen. The house had always had a gas stove and this was exactly the reason why. CJ got a burner lit and put the kettle on.

"We have some instant coffee and a lot of tea." He left out the part about how his mom vastly preferred tea to anything else. Those were the kinds of details he had to keep to himself. He went on, "There's a roast in the slow cooker and potatoes and apple pie in the oven." He lifted the lid and the smell of pot roast filled the air.

"Oh, my God—that smells heavenly," Natalie said. She stepped up next to him and inhaled the fragrant steam.

They worked in silence, assembling the meal. He got down two big bowls and showed her where the tea and the instant coffee were located. He carved the roast and filled their bowls with meat, vegetables and gravy. The kettle whistled and she moved to turn it off.

He was not going to think about how effortlessly she moved around his kitchen. She did not belong here and the fact that he was having to remind himself of this fact approximately once every two-point-four seconds was yet another bad sign. At this point, he wasn't sure he'd recognize a good sign if it bit him on the butt.

It was only when he settled onto the couch with his feet stretched toward the fire that she spoke again. "This is wonderful," she said as she gracefully folded herself into a cross-legged posture on the couch—a solid four feet away from where he sat.

He appreciated that she wasn't starting with another line of questioning—even if she was just trying to soften him up, he was glad there was no full-on assault. That didn't mean he was going to not ask his own questions, however. "How come you don't have anyone waiting for you?"

She didn't answer for a long time—which was understandable, because she was devouring the pot roast. CJ did the same. They ate in silence until she set her bowl to the side. "I could ask the same of you—you're here all alone and Christmas is coming. You don't even have any Christmas decorations up." She looked around his living room. It seemed more barren than normal, with all the pictures gone. "But I won't ask," she said quickly before CJ could remind her of the rules.

He didn't miss the way she avoided answering his question. He glanced up—no ring on her finger. He didn't think she ever wore one—but it was entirely possible that, if she had a ring, she just didn't wear it while she was on TV.

She tucked her hands under her legs. "So, what are we supposed to talk about? I'm not allowed to ask you questions about yourself and so far, I haven't felt comfortable answering any of your questions."

He shrugged. "We don't have to talk about anything. I don't have a problem with silence."

"Oh." Her chin dipped and her shoulders rounded. But then she straightened. "Okay."

He gritted his teeth. At any point, she could stop looking vulnerable and that would be just fine by him. "I don't want to be your lead story. I would rather not talk than have everything I say be twisted around and rebroadcast for mass consumption."

She sighed in resignation, but she didn't drop her gaze this time. "I think it's pretty safe to say that I'm off the clock. Anything we talk about would be off the record."

Like he was going to take her word for *that*. "Patrick Wesley is my father. That's the end of this discussion. I will not allow my personal life to be monetized for someone else's gain."

Besides, outside his parents and apparently Hardwick Beaumont, there was only one other person who knew that Patrick Wesley was not his birth father. CJ had been in love in college—or he thought he had. Really, he had been young and stupid and full of lust and he'd confused all of that with love. But he thought he'd had what his parents had found so he'd told his girlfriend about Hardwick Beaumont being a sperm donor because if he were going to propose to a woman, he wanted her to know the truth about him. He didn't want to spend the rest of his life hiding behind the Wesley name.

He had never forgotten the look on Cindy's face when he'd told her that actually, he was sort of related to the Beaumonts. Her eyes had gone wide and her cheeks had flushed as he'd sat there, waiting for her to say…something. He hadn't been sure what he'd wanted her to say—that it didn't matter, maybe, or that she was sorry his mom was paranoid about the Beaumonts. *Something.* Hardwick Beaumont had still been alive then, although CJ had been twenty-one and beyond his reach.

Cindy hadn't done any of that. After a few moments of stunned silence, she had started to talk about how *wonderful* this was. He was a Beaumont—and the Beaumonts were rich. Why, just think of the wedding that they could have on the Beaumonts' dime! And after the wedding, they could take their proper place in the Beaumont family—and get their proper cut of the Beaumont fortune and on and on and *on*.

That was the moment he realized he'd made a mistake. Panicking, he tried to write the whole thing off as a joke. Of course he wasn't a Beaumont—look at him. The Beaumonts were all sandy and blond—he was brown. It was just… Wishful thinking. Because he'd been bored with being a rancher's son.

He was never sure if Cindy had believed him or not. She'd been pretty mad at him for "teasing" her with all that money. The breakup that followed had been mutual. She wasn't going to get her dream wedding with the bill footed by the Beaumonts and he…

Well, he had learned to keep his mouth shut.

Besides, it had always been easy to ignore the two fundamental lies that made up his life—that Pat Wesley was his father and that his parents had married quietly a year before Pat had brought Bell home with him. It'd been an easy lie to tell—Pat had been finishing up a tour of duty in the army and they told everyone that he and Bell had met and married in secret while he was home on leave. That was why he'd shown up with a wife and a six-month-old that no one else had known about. And because Pat Wesley was an honest, upstanding citizen, everyone had gone along with it.

CJ's mother was brown and Pat Wesley was light. Pat was tall and broad, just like CJ. The fact was, CJ looked like their son. There had never been a question.

The Beaumonts had no bearing on CJ's life. He would've been perfectly happy if he'd never heard the Beaumont name for the rest of his life.

But now he was sitting across from someone who knew—or thought she knew. Which was bad enough.

But what made it worse was that she was looking to capitalize on the knowledge.

She was staring at him, this Natalie Baker. "What do you want me to call you?" she asked.

"My name is CJ Wesley. You can call me CJ."

She held out her hand. "Hi. I'm Natalie."

He hesitated, but when he touched her, palm to palm, a jolt of something traveled between them. He might've thought it was static electricity, but it hit him in all the wrong places. His pulse quickened and warmth—warmth that had nothing to do with the roaring fire only a few feet from them—started at the base of his neck and worked its way down his body.

Oh, no—he knew what this was. *Attraction*. If he wasn't careful, it might blow into something even more difficult to contain—*lust*.

He jerked his hand from hers. "Natalie." Quickly, he got to his feet and gathered up the dishes. "I'll get the pie."

Four

Natalie sat on the couch, trying to make sense of what had happened.

It didn't look like that was a thing that could be done because the longer she stared into the fire, the less she knew about what was going on.

That wasn't entirely true. Once she had thawed out in the shower, her brain worked just fine. She just didn't quite grasp how, in the last two hours, she had gone from being Natalie Baker, host of *A Good Morning with Natalie Baker*, to being a human popsicle, to being…

To being CJ Wesley's unofficial guest.

She felt naked. That feeling had nothing to do with the three separate layers of clothing she was wearing. It had everything to do with the way that man looked at her, his face no longer hidden in the shadows—with the way he asked her why she didn't have anyone waiting for her.

Because she didn't. She could try to lie and say that her producer, Steve, would notice her absence but…it was almost Christmas. They'd been filming segments ahead of schedule and planning to strategically reuse old clips so the crew could have some time off.

She didn't have a single person who would miss her over the next five days. It wasn't like that was a shocking revelation. She'd known damn good and well that it would be yet another Christmas spent alone. She didn't celebrate the holiday. Why would she? The day was nothing but the worst of bad memories.

But somehow, telling CJ that had been… Well, it'd been painful. It had been acknowledging that she was completely alone.

She was more or less completely at CJ's mercy. And he didn't even like her.

But he wasn't taking advantage of the situation. Anyone else would've looked at her half-frozen and seen an opportunity—but not him. Instead, he had clothed her and now he was feeding her. He had gone out of his way to make sure she was comfortable.

He was being entirely too decent. She hadn't realized that people like him existed.

Oh, sure—she knew there were still good humans in the world, the ones who ran soup kitchens and read books during story time at the library. But they didn't come into her world. No, everyone she dealt with wanted something. She didn't know how to talk to someone if it wasn't a negotiation.

And CJ Wesley had made it abundantly clear that he didn't want to negotiate. She didn't have anything he wanted and he wasn't interested in giving up anything to her.

They had reached an impasse. In less than two hours.

Awareness prickled over her skin the moment he entered the room, even though he was padding around silently in thick sheepskin-lined moccasins. There was something about the way the air changed around him. For all of his decency and grudging niceness, CJ Wesley was a powerful force to be reckoned with.

"Good," he said as he crossed in front of her and sat back down on the couch, then handed her a plate overflowing with what looked like the best apple pie she'd ever seen.

She wasn't sure what he was calling *good*—the pie or the fact that she hadn't wandered off to unearth his family secrets.

"Thank you," she said. "You don't have to serve me."

There—the muscle in his jaw twitched just as he said, "It's no problem. I'm happy to do it."

She twisted her lips to one side, trying not to smile at him. "You're lying. But I appreciate it anyway."

He paused, a forkful of pie halfway to his mouth. "I'm not lying." The twitch was harder to see this time, because he was sliding his fork into his mouth.

But she saw it anyway.

"You have a tell. Did you know that?"

He avoided answering her for several long minutes, so she dug in to the pie. Sweet merciful heavens, it was even better than it smelled. Homemade and warm, the apples perfectly spiced and the crust flaky. The roast had been excellent—but this?

Maybe she had died in the snow. She'd frozen to death and this was actually heaven. Curled up on the couch with a sexy, grouchy cowboy and the best apple pie in the world.

"This is fabulous," she all but moaned around her third forkful.

"Thanks, my—" He bit off the word. "Thanks," he said again.

She surreptitiously glanced at his hand—no ring, no tan line, either. Aside from the clothes she was wearing—which were baggy and not exactly in the height of fashion—there were no other signs of women in this house. At least not since she'd taken her shower. She was pretty sure there had been pictures on the wall and now there weren't. But she had been too cold to study them when she'd originally walked through the house.

No, CJ didn't have a wife. Which meant that this pie had probably been made by his mom. The very woman that Natalie had been stalking through court records for months.

It was equally obvious that he was absolutely not going to acknowledge his mother's existence.

Natalie Baker, morning television host, would have pressed for details. But the pie was too good and the fire was too warm and she just didn't want to. If CJ were right, she would have several days to work on him. But not right now. Her stomach was full and she was feeling warm and drowsy—well, parts of her were. Other parts of her were way too attuned to the man sitting three feet away from her.

"I don't have a tell," he said suddenly.

"Yes, you do." She shot him a little smile—it didn't even feel forced. She was teasing him and there was something about it that felt okay. Like she could tease him just a little and he wouldn't throw her out.

He was trying to look mean. "No, I don't." She lifted her eyebrows and, still grinning at him, nodded sympathetically. He held her gaze for a moment and then slumped back against the couch. "What is it?"

She sat her plate to the side and leaned forward. When she lifted her hand toward his face, he tensed. "Easy," she told him as his eyes widened—and darkened. "I'm just going to show you this." She laid the tips of her fingers against the muscle of his jaw. "Call this an…experiment, if you will."

The edge of his beard pricked the pads of her fingers and the question that she had been going to ask—are you Hardwick Beaumont's son?—died on her lips. She knew what would happen. He would shut down on her or tell her to stop talking or get off the couch. She didn't want that to happen.

So her mind spun for a question that he wouldn't want to answer truthfully but wouldn't be the end of the conversation, either. "Did your mom make the pie?"

The muscle under her fingertips moved. "No."

"Did you feel that?" She gave his cheek a gentle pat. "Right here. Every time you tell a lie, a muscle twitches."

"I don't believe you." But he hadn't pushed her hand away. Instead, he sat still as a stone—a boulder. But not the angry, immovable boulder he'd been earlier. There was something cautious about him now.

She pulled her fingers away—but only to pick up his hand and push his palm against the side of his face. "Pay attention," she told him and was more than amused when he sat up straighter. She didn't pull her palm away as she held his hand to his face. "Do you watch my show?"

"Yes. Sometimes." Then he said, "I didn't feel anything."

"Were you being honest?" Because suddenly, that

seemed very important. Obviously, she knew that he knew who she was. He had known from the very first.

"Yes."

"Okay," she told him. "So you can see that nothing happened when you told the truth." She tilted her head to one side and his eyes widened. *What?* She hadn't done anything. She needed another question. A safe question. "Did you lie to me in the feed store about who Pat Wesley was?"

"No," he answered quickly. Then his eyes widened. "Crap."

Reluctantly, she let her hand drop. "See? That's your tell."

He was rubbing the side of his face. "I would deny everything, but I get the feeling you would know immediately."

She laughed. Not a coquettish giggle, but an honest laugh. "I bet you were a Boy Scout and everything, weren't you?"

"I don't have to answer that." But instead of sounding irritated, one corner of his mouth curved up into a small, blink-and-you-miss-it smile. All she could do was stare at him as the firelight played over his face. He was so handsome it was almost unfair. It certainly overruled every one of her self-preservation instincts.

She did not normally go for rough-and-tumble

men. Mostly because they had very little to offer her, beyond occasionally great sex.

But CJ Wesley was something else entirely. Rough and grouchy, but with a core of human decency that was more surprising than anything else—and all wrapped up in muscles. Suddenly, she knew that if he turned that smile on full power and aimed it directly at her, she wasn't going to make it.

This was *terrible*, she realized with a start. She was actually starting to like him. Sexual attraction was one thing, but this? This was something else entirely.

Quickly, she reminded herself of the stakes. He was just being nice to her because... Because it was better to keep your enemies closer than your friends and there was no mistaking the fact that she was his enemy. If she made the mistake of confusing niceness with affection, then she really *was* stupid.

Besides, he was not interested. But the moment that thought occurred to her, she wished she'd asked "Are you attracted to me?" instead of the question about the pie. Because what would he have said?

His gaze slid toward her. "I'm not the only one with a tell, you know."

She highly doubted that. She was experienced in bending the truth—which was a nice way of saying she had learned to lie through her teeth. "Nice try, but I don't think that's going to work."

He turned his entire body to her, propping up one

of his legs on the couch. The distance between them got smaller. "You don't think so?"

She arranged her face into a mask of casualness. "I know so. Don't forget who I am."

He stared at her for a long moment. The back of Natalie's neck began to prickle and she was terribly afraid she was about to blush.

"I haven't forgotten," he said and he sounded so serious about it.

"I'm very important," she reminded him because that was the sort of thing she *had* to say.

His eyes widened. "There."

"What?"

"The way you swallowed. That's your tell."

It was suddenly a little more difficult to breathe, but she couldn't let him know that. Instead, she looked at him doubtfully. "First off, you didn't even ask me a question—ergo, how can you tell if I was lying? And second off, how do you know I didn't just have a bit of apple pie stuck in my throat?"

He notched an eyebrow at her and angled his body toward hers. In all reality, there probably was still a solid two and a half feet between them. But that's not what it felt like. The air seemed to crackle. Or it could have been the fire. "All right, I'll ask a question. Are you seeing anyone?"

She considered lying, but she didn't. "No."

He tilted his head to one side as he appraised her. "Why won't anyone miss you?"

Somehow, she wasn't surprised that was the question he went with. She was pulling her punches because it seemed like the polite thing for a semi-involuntary guest to do—but he had no such social obligations.

"People will miss me," she told him. "Trust me, people pay attention to me."

He smirked. It was not a reassuring gesture. "You don't even know you did it, do you? You swallowed. You pause and then you swallow and then you tell a bold-faced lie." With that, he turned back to the fire.

She should let it go. He was getting uncomfortably close to some basic truths about her and she didn't want him to. But she couldn't help it. "People do pay attention to me, you know? I'm something of a celebrity."

To her horror, he hitched up a hip and pulled her phone out of his pocket. He didn't have her password—there was no way in hell she was going to give it to him—but the Twitter notifications were rolling over the screen. "Yes, I see that. What did you tweet to get—" He paused, his eyes popping wide. "Do you know what these people are saying?"

She couldn't watch him read all the horrible, terrible things people were saying about her, so she closed her eyes. "Probably. But they pay attention to me."

He looked at her like she was absolutely nuts. And here, in the warm safety of the Wesley family home, it did seem a bit crazy. "You can't seriously want them to say— Good Lord, is that even legal?" He glanced at her, looking more worried by the second. "This isn't right. People shouldn't say— Oh, that's just disgusting."

The embarrassment was too much. She lunged at him, trying to grab her phone. He easily held it out of reach, damn his long arms. Instead, all she accomplished was lurching into the side of his shoulder.

"Put it away," she said, her cheeks burning. "Just...put it away."

He glanced at the screen one more time before he pushed the button at the top. The phone powered down until it was blissfully, safely black. "You should save your battery, anyway." But he didn't give her the phone. Instead, he slid it back into his pocket. "Do I want to know what you said that garnered such evil replies?" His face hardened. "Was it about me?"

"No."

He looked at her for a long time. "Was it about a Beaumont?"

This time, she noticed it. She swallowed just before she opened her mouth. So she shut her mouth a second time. He was studying her way too closely— like he could see beneath her TV personality, beneath the aura of untouchability that she cultivated. He could see *into* her and she was suddenly terrified he would realize there was nothing really there.

"So, that's a yes, then."

She didn't know what to say, so she said nothing. If he could hide behind silence, so could she.

The moments stretched into minutes and the minutes kept right on stretching as they sat there, a few feet separating them, both watching the fire. She didn't know what time it was. It was near total darkness outside. The shadows played over the corners of the room and once again, she felt small.

The longer she sat there, the more she realized something—aside from her father, who accused her of lying with every other breath, no one had ever noticed that she had a tell before. She was creative with reality on a daily basis and aside from the people on social media, no one ever called her on it. Certainly not to her face. No one had ever pressed her for the truth before. Not even her father, who never believed a single word she said.

Why was that? She was afraid to look too closely for the answer.

Unexpectedly, CJ asked, "Why?"

He didn't expand on that. He didn't have to.

"It's my job. It's how the game is played." People like Matthew Beaumont understood that. People like CJ Wesley? They didn't understand it at all.

"It's a lousy game, if you don't mind me saying so."

Almost against her will, she smiled. There was something so…gentlemanly about him. She wasn't sure she'd ever met a man she could call a gentleman. "It's not all bad," she said, willing herself to believe that was the truth.

The moment stretched again and then he stood up so abruptly that she jolted in her seat. "I'll bring in more wood from the mudroom. Don't move."

"I won't." She owed him that much. She had made a promise and, for once in her life, she was going to keep it. As long as she was a guest in his house, she would not pry.

She felt the air shift and a cold draft blew through the living room before CJ walked back in, his arms overflowing with logs. He carried them as if they weighed nothing at all and when he crouched down in front of the fire, she got a good look at his ass. As he messed around with the fire, she studied his body. Lord, he was built. Okay, so maybe she was starting to like him. A gruff cowboy who was also a gentleman? A man with rough hands who liked apple pie?

They were stuck here for several days. She knew one way to pass the time.

He stood and dusted off his hands before turning back to her. Her breath caught in her throat as he looked down at her, backlit by the fire. *Strong*—that was the word that bubbled up through the building lust in her mind. He was strong and safe and confident. What would he be like? Was he the kind of gentleman who would put her first or was he like all the other guys—quick, selfish. *Lousy.* God, she was so tired of having lousy sex and then feeling nothing but...hollow after.

Maybe it would be different with him. She wanted it to be—more than that, she wanted *him* to be different. A thought flitted through her mind—maybe *she* could be different with him.

She pushed herself off the couch and stepped onto his pallet.

His hands dropped to his sides and he straightened. "What are you doing?"

She stepped into him and touched his cheek, right where his muscles would twitch. He was warm and solid and Natalie knew he could pick her up and carry her anywhere he wanted to. "Thanking you," she said, wrapping her other arm around his waist and molding herself to his body.

Just the contact of her breasts to his chest—never mind how many layers of clothes were in the way—was enough to make her knees weaken. Her nipples tightened and she exhaled in anticipation. She could be someone else while she was stranded with him. Someone *better*. Someone who got what she wanted. He was hot and hard and she wanted to rip the shirt off of him and test each and every single muscle. What other parts of him twitched?

She lifted herself on her tiptoes, close enough for her cheek to brush over his beard before he put his hands on her hips and forcibly pushed her away. "Don't," he said, his voice thick with strain.

His hands were still on her hips—but now there was a solid foot of space between them. She blinked up at him. "Why not? You're being wonderful and I—"

"For God's sake, Natalie—*don't*." Now he sounded angry at her. "You don't owe me anything and I don't owe you anything and…and…" He let go of her and instead of sinking to the floor, he pushed her back. She stood there for a moment, confused.

He wanted her, she realized. He didn't like her, but he wanted her.

She could work with that. "CJ," she began in what she thought was a sultry voice.

His eyes snapped up and he glared at her.

She faltered. "Don't you…don't you want me?"

He jerked his head to the side and quickly stepped around her. "This is not happening." She blinked at him as he kicked off his moccasins, his back to her. "Go to sleep, Natalie. And don't try that again."

"Why not? Am I that—"

"There is absolutely nothing that's going to happen between us. You know it. I know it. I'm not having any part of my life made public and there's no guarantee that anything I say or do with you won't wind up on television." He finally turned to face her, his eyes narrow and his shoulders bunched up under his sweater. "It's bedtime. Go to sleep." There was a hard edge to his voice that made her chest tight.

"Oh. Okay. I…" She swallowed. "All right."

She stepped around him, careful not to touch him, and laid down on the couch. But sleep didn't come.

Instead, she stared into the fire and replayed all the ways she'd made a complete and total fool of herself in the last twelve hours. In the last lifetime.

Just as she finally started to drift, she realized something—when she'd asked him if he wanted her, he'd turned away.

He'd hidden his tell.

Five

He was going to regret this.

That was nothing new. CJ already regretted the moment Natalie Baker had walked off his television screen and into his life. But, as he stared down at her sleeping form, he knew he was going to regret what he was about to do more than anything else.

Even more than he regretted pushing her away last night.

To be honest, only parts of him regretted that. He knew that keeping a hard wall between him and the woman out to expose him as one of the lost Beaumont bastards was the only thing to do.

But try telling that to his erection.

So what he needed to do now—which he was

going to regret, also—was keep them both busy.
Idle hands were the devil's workshop, after all. He
couldn't take any more sitting around and talking
to her and he especially couldn't give her another
chance to press her body against his and look up
into his eyes and…

A very hard wall. "Natalie."

She was dead asleep. The vulnerability that
called to him yesterday? It was magnified a hundred times right now. In sleep, she didn't just look
soft and vulnerable—she looked innocent. Without
the calculating shift to her eyes and the hardened
jaw tight and ready for battle, she was a completely
different woman. Sweet, even.

"Natalie. Wake up."

Her brow creased, so he knew she heard him. But
still, her eyes didn't open.

He sat on his heels in front of her and held a cup
of coffee directly under her nose. But he didn't touch
her. He didn't dare brush the strands of hair that had
come loose from her ponytail away from her cheek
and he didn't dare stroke his thumb over her cheek to
coax her awake. If he touched her, he might be lost.

"Wake up," he repeated and he blew on the coffee so the steam hit her in the face.

"What time is it?" she asked without opening her
eyes.

"Six thirty." Then he waited for her reaction to
this. He wasn't quite sure what he expected.

She stretched like a cat in a sunbeam and pushed herself into a sitting position. "That late?" She blinked at him, tilting her head from side to side. "Wow."

He stared at her and offered up the coffee. "Is that a joke?"

She took the cup in her hand. "I normally get up at four thirty every morning. I'm at the studio by five thirty for hair and makeup and to prepare for the show." She took a sip and CJ forced himself to look somewhere else—anywhere else, except for where her lips were touching the edge of the cup.

Those lips had almost touched his last night. All he'd had to do was turn his head ever so slightly and…

"I get up at four in the summer," he told her for no reason at all—except because he was trying not to stare at her. "I don't meet too many people who get up that early who aren't ranchers."

She cupped the coffee in her hands and sighed with what sounded like happiness. When she lifted her gaze to his, it took everything he had not to lean forward and kiss the taste of coffee off her lips. "Are you saying that we might actually have something in common?"

He stood, putting some distance between them. *No kissing. End of discussion.* "We have things to do today. We need to get moving."

She stared up at him as if he had suddenly started

speaking French. Of course, someone like her probably did speak French. He was fluent in Spanish—not that he was going to tell her that. "We...do?" She looked around, her head moving slowly. She was not fully awake yet. "Did the snowstorm end?"

"No. It's still going. I think the wind has died down a bit, but there's probably about eighteen inches outside. We'll have over two feet before it's done."

Something in her face shifted. Was it fear? Resignation? She'd tried to seduce him last night. Was the thought of being trapped here for another few days that unpleasant to her? "What are we going to do?"

He stepped back and threw another log on the fire. "I was thinking about it. Last night you asked me what we were going to talk about and I made a decision." Flames licked along the new wood and then caught. "We're not going to talk about the past and there's no point in talking about the future. So what we're going to do is focus on the now." He peeked back over his shoulder to see that she was looking at him, utter confusion written all over her face. "It's Christmas, Natalie. And I think we need a little Christmas."

Her eyes brightened. "Right this very minute?"

"Yes," he said, feeling a smile take hold of his face. "We need a little Christmas. But the same rules apply. You won't ask me about anything and I won't tell you. Also, you should know—if I can get my snowmobile out, I'm going to town on Christmas

Eve. There's a big party there every year and this year I'm Santa. The roads in town might be cleared, so you can have someone come get you." The twinkle in her eyes faded. "You can get your car later."

She dropped her gaze to the coffee cup and took a slow, steady breath. "You really don't look very much like Santa."

"Looks aren't everything." Before she could respond to that, he clapped his hands. "Normally, I'd already have decorated some by now but things have been a little…different this year." As in, he had been busy trying to keep Natalie Baker from finding out who he was—and failing somewhat spectacularly. The thought of his father's two great lies suddenly being exposed hadn't exactly put CJ in the holiday mood.

Even though the room was still a washed-out gray, he could see the color in her cheeks deepen. She was the thing that was different this year—there was no getting around that obvious fact—but he still felt bad reminding her of it. "Come on."

"Hold the light," he told her. It'd taken twenty minutes to get breakfast squared away, but now they were downstairs, poking around in the bins of decorations.

When his mom had been here for Christmas, every square inch of the house had been decorated until the entire place was red, green and shimmery silver. Bell

Wesley loved shining tinsel and, even though Dad hated the stuff, he let her go wild. Claimed that what made his wife happy made him happy. Therefore, the house had always been completely decorated from the Day of the Dead until January first. They had storage containers stacked four high and three wide for all of the holiday decorations.

CJ wouldn't get all of them out. First off, he didn't really want to drag out all of the Mexican decorations. The papel picado—the colored paper cut in lace patterns—and the ornaments of tiny piñatas and sombreros would be dead giveaways. But things like his mother's manger scenes and Virgin Mary ornaments—those were fine. "Can you shed a little light over here?"

Natalie adjusted the beam. "This is a lot," she said in amazement. "Is this all Christmas?"

"Maybe seventy percent of it." He began pulling the appropriate bins—each labeled with tags like Manger, Lights and Wreaths—and setting them to the side. He stopped in front of a bin labeled CJ's Handmade Ornaments. Crap, he'd forgotten about that one. If they weren't talking about the past, he didn't want to pull out the collection of ornaments he had been making for his mother, one per year, every year for the last thirty-two years. The early ones were nothing more than little handprints in clay or scribbled paper trees with yarn strung through the top.

He hadn't even given her this year's ornament

before they left—a wooden star he'd cut on his drill press. It sat out in the barn, finished except for some sanding and maybe another coat of lacquer.

He must've stared at that bin too long because when he finally moved to pull it off the shelf, Natalie stepped forward and put her hand on his shoulder. "You don't have to," she said in a soft voice.

He tensed. Even through all the layers of clothing, he could feel the warmth from her touch, just like he'd felt last night. "Don't have to do what?"

"That." The beam of the flashlight bounced off the bin. "You don't have to show me those."

He turned to stare at her, although there wasn't much to see in the basement. "Don't you want to know?"

She swallowed, then appeared to catch herself. Her mouth twisted off into a half frown. "I do," she said, looking frustrated, "but I don't."

CJ stared at her. He had no hopes of ever understanding her, none whatsoever, but still, times like these, when she almost made sense... And then didn't.

She rolled her eyes. "It's called plausible deniability, CJ. If you don't show me the ornaments, I don't have to ask about them and you don't have to lie. Then, if anyone asks me if I've seen any of CJ's homemade Christmas memories, I can say *no*, I did not."

See, that was a prime example of her making

sense and no sense at the same time. He understood what she was saying... But the fact that the woman who had stalked him for three weeks was the one saying it? *That* didn't make any sense. "You're not going to pry?"

This time, he didn't see her swallow at all. "I gave you my word I wouldn't."

Abruptly, she turned off the flashlight. CJ tensed, but she didn't make another pass at him. Instead, she leaned down and picked up one of the bins. "This basement is cold," she said, hauling the bin up the stairs.

He was never going to understand women. Specifically, this woman. Because everything she had just said was completely at odds with everything she had said prior to this. Was this some sort of persuasion technique he wasn't familiar with? Reverse psychology, maybe? Was she hoping that, by telling him she didn't want him to share secrets, he would be more likely to start blabbing?

He'd never much been one for psychology. So, as dangerous as it might be, he was going to take her at face value. She wanted plausible deniability? Fine. He would give her all the plausible deniability she could handle.

It took everything Natalie had not to ask questions. Because obviously, some of these decorations had been in his family for years. Decades, even. The manger scene that he arranged on the mantel over the fireplace? It was so old that the baby Jesus's face had been rubbed off and one of the donkeys was missing a leg.

The sleigh bells CJ told her to hang on the front doorknob—which was freezing cold—looked even older than the manger. But the silk poinsettia arrangement that she set in the middle of the big dining room table, that was newer.

Then he pulled out one of those things that she'd never known the name for—it was shaped like a Christmas tree but it had candles and a little propeller at the top. If you lit the candles, the heat turned the propeller. It was like a Christmas tree crossed with a helicopter. She had always wanted one and had once, when she was a little girl, asked Santa for one.

Her parents had told her Santa wasn't real but Natalie had held out hope that maybe, just maybe, Santa existed and that she'd been a good girl. She'd tried so hard, hoping that if she could just act right, everything would be good. Or, at the very least, Santa would bring her a present, one that said she was worth something special.

Foolish childhood delusions. And she'd gotten so upset when her special Christmas toy hadn't appeared that she'd cried. And that was when her mother had walked out because Natalie had ruined Christmas for everyone.

Still, it was exciting to see a Christmas helicopter

in person, Natalie thought, dragging herself back to the present. CJ had said it himself—the past didn't matter. Not today.

And since CJ seemed to have a lot of candles, maybe they could light it up and she could watch the wheels spin. "I always wanted one of these when I was a kid," she said, stacking the layers on top of each other. "Where do you want it?"

"Here," CJ said, pointing to a side table. "You didn't have one?"

"No." Carefully, she set the assembled whirly thing on the table. "I hope we'll be able to light it. I always wanted to see one in action."

She could feel CJ looking at her. He did that often. Maybe too often. Was he thinking about the way she'd thrown herself at him last night? Was he regretting saving her life and bringing her into his home? She was trying so hard not to make him regret it.

"Yes?" she asked as she turned to face him. There it was again, the look that told her he was trying to figure her out.

"I think we got that thing when I was a kid," he offered. But even as he said it, he looked mad at her again. "What kinds of decorations did you have growing up?"

"Oh." She turned back to the bin and pulled out a bag full of beautiful, hand-tied bows made of lustrous, sheer ribbons. Someone had put a lot of love into those bows—the same love that went into the apple pie, she'd bet. "Where would you like these?"

She felt him step closer a moment before he touched her hand. "Do you celebrate Christmas?" When she didn't answer right away, he added, "One of my best friends from college is Jewish. Hanukkah, the eight nights, the candles—it's all really interesting," he added, as if he were trying to make her feel better for not having Christmas.

"We aren't Jewish." Being Jewish would give her a reason to avoid Christmas, but it wouldn't have made those years of miserable holiday seasons any more bearable. "I've seen pictures," she said, helpless to stop the words that were inexplicably rolling off of her tongue. He was sharing so much with her that it suddenly felt wrong not to share anything with him. "Back when my mom was still with us, there's a picture of me and her and Dad all sitting in front of the tree with ornaments and lights and presents and *everything*."

Unexpectedly, her throat closed up. She had that picture in a box under her bed. The one time the Baker family had been happy—and she was too young to remember it. Instead of memories, all she had was a picture. "So I know we used to celebrate it."

The words hung in the quiet room and mortification swamped her. It was the truth—but that didn't make it sound any less sad.

She dug in the bin again and turned up a pair of snow globes. "Where do you want these?" she asked, ignoring the way her voice cracked.

"I'm sorry you lost your mom," he said gruffly.

This whole situation was so ridiculous that she couldn't help but laugh. "She's not dead. At least, I don't think she is. She just...left me. Us," she quickly amended.

But she hadn't been quick enough. "Natalie."

Damn it all, she should have lied. She made the executive decision that the snow globes belonged on opposite sides of the mantel. "What do you think?" Before he could answer, she dug back into the bin and came out with two cut-tin candleholders. With a lit candle inside, they would throw the shadows of trees and stars and snowflakes onto the walls. "These are perfect. We're already using candles," she said brightly.

"Natalie," he said again, this time with more force.

But she couldn't stop. She couldn't think about what she had just said out loud. She had never once admitted to anyone that her mother had left her because she'd ruined Christmas—or that her father had never celebrated the holiday after that.

As far as Natalie knew, Julie Baker had never seen either her daughter or her husband again. Now that she was an adult, Natalie knew her father had been a major factor in Mom's departure. The man was impossible to please and harder to live with.

But that realization had come later. Natalie had spent *years* with her mother's parting words ringing in her ears.

She focused all of her energy on the bins of decorations. The next thing she pulled out was plastic mistletoe with a bell hanging out of the bottom. "Where should I hang—"

"Natalie." CJ grabbed her by the shoulders and spun her around.

"What?" She looked into his eyes—*hazel, definitely hazel in this light*—and realized there was nowhere to hide. He could see her.

It was terrifying.

"Your mother left you?"

Natalie hated that prickling at the corner of her eyes, so she ignored it. "It's not a big deal." Too late, she realized she had swallowed. Hell, if she were going to lie, she might as well go big. "It's fine," she assured him, forcing a big sunny smile to her face.

"And after she left, you didn't celebrate Christmas?"

"Oh, sure we did. In…" She swallowed. "In our own way."

His mouth twisted. "You're not a very good liar, you know?"

His comment was so ridiculous she didn't know what to do—except laugh. "Actually, I am," she told him. "I can't remember the last time I was this honest." With someone else *or* with herself. That realization made her laugh even harder.

He did not laugh with her. "Is this a trick?" he asked, but his voice wasn't angry. Neither were his eyes. He was staring at her with such intensity that it made her want to squirm. If anyone else had looked at her like he did, she would know that sooner rather than later, they would wind up back at her place, naked and panting.

But CJ Wesley wasn't like anyone else.

"A trick?" It took a few moments for her to make sense of what he'd just said. Then it hit her.

He thought this entire thing—the damsel in distress, not having anyone to call for Christmas, even her hysteria—was an act.

Her giggles died in the back of her throat. Is that how he saw her?

She deserved that, she knew. If anyone else had accused her of playing mind games, she would've smiled softly and said something outrageous—something to prove them right while still maintaining what little dignity she had left. Dignity she didn't have right now. For once, she wished that she'd kept her big mouth shut.

"It's all right," she said and was horrified to hear her voice crack. "I mean, come on—I'm nothing but a whiny, spoiled-rotten little brat, right?" The words spilled out of her before she could stop. "I ruin everything. I always have."

She didn't know what she expected him to do with this—because she was, in fact, ruining both his Christmas and his life—but suddenly, she was crushed against his chest. His arms enveloped her—he was so strong and sure of who he was and what he was doing.

She tried to hold back because she didn't deserve this hug. His anger, his mockery, his criticism—yes. Not this tenderness.

But he didn't let her go.

"It's okay," he whispered, low and close to her ear and damn it all, she sank into his warmth. He smelled of wood and smoke, of warmth and safety. She was safe in his arms and if she couldn't blink fast enough to erase the prickling in her eyes, well, that was okay, too.

She shouldn't want this—the way his arms felt around her waist, the way her face fit against the crook of his neck. She shouldn't want the way his hands were rubbing up and down her back, relaxing her and pushing her closer to him—closer than she'd been last night. But he wasn't taking anything. Instead, he was offering comfort—the comfort of his body, of *him*.

Comfort was perilously close to pity and she didn't want his pity. She didn't want him thinking she needed him at all. She was Natalie Baker and that meant something. She took care of herself. She had for years.

Still, it was several minutes before she could bring herself to push away from him. "Are you always this damn decent?" she asked, rubbing her cheeks with the cuff of her sleeve.

A long moment passed where he wasn't touching her and he wasn't talking. Finally, when she could barely take another second of it, he said, "Just doing what anyone would do for a friend."

"That's just it," she snapped at him. She was angry now. In theory, she was supposed to be breaking down CJ Wesley—and the opposite was happening. She was starting to like him and if that happened, she might as well kiss her morning show goodbye. "No one is this good and decent and kind and nice, don't you see that? No one is." He made a motion toward her, but she backed away. Her legs touched the couch and she sat with an undignified *thump.* "You are not normal and we're not friends."

The words weren't very insulting and they did exactly zero damage to him. "I don't think you're whiny and I'm not sure that you're such a spoiled brat," he said gently. She cringed to hear the words spoken aloud again. "I think you're…"

"What?" she demanded. If she made him mad, he wouldn't pity her. "Delusional? Scheming? Conniving—that's a good one. One of my favorites."

He shook his head. "I think you're lonely."

She had to laugh—*had* to. Because she could absolutely not sit here and cry. "Really, CJ—me?" She scoffed as best she could. "Please. Do you know what my market share is in morning television ratings?" As if that had anything to do with loneliness. "And what about you?" she quickly added because she didn't want him to expound upon this flash of insight. "Why the hell aren't you married? Because you should be. You are gorgeous and decent and well-off and you don't play games. Why don't you have a wife and kids? Or even a husband and some kids?"

Now it was his turn to blink at her. But he didn't cuss her out or tell her to go to hell. "You know why."

She did? Really, she didn't know that much about him except...

Except she was sure that his father was Hardwick Beaumont.

"So?" she asked in confusion. "It's not like you've got a third nipple or a vestigial tail—right?"

The corner of his mouth twitched—an almost smile. "You mean, something useless and left over from the past that has no impact on my life anymore, but that people still find fascinating?"

"That is the definition of *vestigial*." It was such a relief to be off the topic of her that she kept going. This was as close as he'd come to admitting the truth about his birth father. But they weren't actually discussing the Beaumonts. They were maintaining the aura of plausible deniability. Somehow that made it okay. She hoped, anyway. "But I don't see why that would keep you from being with someone."

He winced. "Let's just say that having a vestigial organ—that's important to some people. And you never know which people it's going to be important to, so you don't tell anyone about this *organ*." Her gaze dipped down to a different organ, but before she could wonder about *that*, he turned to face the fire. "And then let's say that you fall in love—or you think you do. And you're convinced that this person you've fallen in love with doesn't care about vestigial organs. You're convinced that this person can see past that imperfection. So you tell them about it and it turns out it matters." His voice dropped. "It matters a lot."

She regarded him for a long moment as she thought over his disclosure. Unexpectedly, shame hit her low and hard. He was right. It was important—if it weren't, she wouldn't be here. And if things had gone according to plan, she would have been telling everyone else in the broadcast market that it mattered more than anything else they might hear on another channel.

She felt ill. "But if this vestigial organ was so important to some people, why did they keep quiet once they found out about it? Because if it was important to them, they wouldn't keep it to themselves. Trust me on that one."

That was how she made her living—people knew something they weren't supposed to and they just couldn't keep their mouths shut. More than that, though, they were looking to capitalize on their knowledge. Knowing something that other people didn't know was exciting. Knowing you could get paid for it was *power*.

He adjusted the angle of one of the snow globes on the mantel. "You lie, of course. You tell them it was a practical joke, that you were just pulling their leg. You laugh it off. And then, a few weeks after that, you break up with them." He glanced over his shoulder at her. "They never figured it out, because they never noticed that you had a tell. And then you decide not to tell anyone else."

For some reason, that bit about the tell made her smile. But it didn't last. Because no one else had ever figured out her tell, either. All those people watching her and following her online every day—and none of them had seen that simple truth. Not like CJ had.

She looked him over again. Years of not telling anyone? They weren't that far away from Denver— an hour, maybe. The Beaumonts and their soap-opera lives would be unavoidable. And he said *she* was lonely.

"She couldn't tell? Because I can. I can see the vestigial organ in you."

He turned to face her head-on again. "My dad—"

"Pat?"

He nodded, politely ignoring her interruption. "He's six-two. He's a little bit Scot and more than a little Irish. Eyes that aren't quite blue, aren't quite green. When he was a kid, he was strawberry-blond—although his hair's darkened and now he's a light-brown kind of guy."

"You look like him." True, he could've been describing Hardwick Beaumont—but that would explain why no one would have seen the Beaumont in him if he also looked like Patrick Wesley.

"I look like both my parents." It was such a simple statement—and nothing twitched in any of his muscles.

A new feeling—unfamiliar—blew up faster than a winter storm. Guilt. Because she knew what was going to happen next.

Oh, sure—maybe for the rest of the Christmas holiday things would be quiet. But after that?

"I'm so sorry, CJ."

His brow wrinkled. "For what?"

"For finding you."

CJ exhaled heavily and came over to the couch. He slumped down in it, a couple of feet still between them. But it wasn't uncomfortable, that space. "You're not ruining my Christmas," he told her. "So stop worrying about it."

"But…"

He shook his head. "Natalie, I told you—we're dealing with the present today." Never mind the fact that they hadn't actually been doing that at all, beyond thinking about where to put the snow globes.

"The future isn't going anywhere and I'll deal with it when the time comes."

So he understood, then. She had found him, after all. She'd spent weeks asking questions about Carlos Julián and Isabel Santino, about Beaumont's bastard son. She had made the connection and in doing so, she'd paved the way for others to make the same connection, too.

And he knew it.

"Why aren't you madder at me?" She stared at him, but he kept his gaze on the fire. "You should be furious, you know." He should've left her in the snow. It probably wouldn't have solved anything in the long run, but she deserved his anger.

She wasn't going to get it. That much was already clear, and it became clearer when he just shrugged. "I don't know," he said in an amused tone, as if he couldn't believe he wasn't more upset with her, too. "Maybe…" He glanced at her and forced an awkward smile. For a moment, she thought he was going to finish that statement.

But then he stood and nudged a nearly empty bin with his toe. "We should get this mess cleaned up and then I'll see if I can get out to the generator."

They finished decorating and carried the empty bins back downstairs. The whole time, Natalie tried to figure out why he wasn't raging at her. She hadn't exactly destroyed his life—but she had upended it, at the very least. She'd had people threaten to do all sorts of horrible things to her for far less than this.

But if they were threatening her or talking about how stupid she was, at least she knew they were paying attention. That was how the world worked.

Or it had, before she had met CJ Wesley. Finally, someone who should be legitimately angry with her, someone who had plenty of opportunity to exact revenge, and what had he done?

Saved her life. Kept her safe and warm. Made sure she was comfortable and fed. Hell, he'd even let her celebrate Christmas with him. He had offered her the simple reassurance of a hug when she'd let down her guard and accidentally thought about her childhood.

And all he asked in return was that she not pry. There had been no threats, no physical or sexual intimidation. Just kindness.

She wished she'd never found him.

Six

"How much do you think we got?" He and Natalie were standing by the big picture window, staring at a world muffled by white.

"Two and a half feet, maybe a little more. That," he said, pointing toward a tiny mound just a little higher than the rest of the snow, "is your car."

"Wow," Natalie said, sounding awestruck.

He snorted. She'd be lucky if she got her car back before March, CJ thought as he watched the moon finally appear out from behind the last straggling clouds. Suddenly the world was bathed in a bright, crystal white.

"It's so peaceful out here." She crossed her arms and shivered.

They were far from the fire, but neither of them moved away from the window. He fought the urge to wrap his arm around her shoulders and pull her closer. "You say that now, but that's just because the cabin fever hasn't hit yet."

She gave him a sideways glance. "Is that going to be a problem?"

Hell, yes it was going to be a problem. It was a problem already. They'd killed an afternoon decorating the living room. Even then, they hadn't managed to stick to the here and now. Instead, he'd held her and she'd asked about third nipples. What the hell would happen tomorrow?

Would they get bored? Boredom couldn't be good.

He knew the cure for cabin fever—it would be to peel her out of all of those clothes, curl his body around hers and spend hours getting lost in her.

And he couldn't do it. He wanted to, though. It was probably a normal thing for two consenting adults who were attracted to each other and stranded together during a Christmas blizzard to spend some time working through sexual frustration, right?

But that wasn't the only reason why he wanted to pull her into his arms. Part of it was the devastated look on her face when he had said she was lonely. He actually wasn't sure if she was or wasn't. But saying it out loud made him realize something.

He was lonely. Aside from Cindy back in college, he hadn't told anyone about being a Beaumont—

because he hadn't given himself the chance to do that. He had kept to himself for years.

Long, lonely years. All because he didn't trust another person with the truth. He assumed that whoever he told would react much the way Cindy had—with shock, quickly followed by greed.

But Natalie? He hadn't even had to tell her—she'd figured it out. She knew the truth—and it *was* true. There was no point in lying about it because she would be able to tell.

She knew that Hardwick Beaumont was his father and…

It wasn't like she didn't care. She wouldn't have gotten this far if she didn't care. But she wasn't acting like he was her personal bank account and she was hell-bent on making a withdrawal. Instead, she had apologized. And he had no reason to believe it wasn't a sincere apology.

He still didn't want to be a featured segment on her show. But today she'd made him realize how damnably exhausting it was to keep other people's secrets and he didn't want to do that anymore, either. Hell, he didn't know what he wanted.

So he focused on the present. "Tomorrow, when the sun's out, I'll get the generator going. If I can get to the barn, I'll be able to get the snowmobile out. We can go for a ride after I feed my horses."

She beamed up at him and damn if it didn't make him feel warm inside. "Really?"

"Yep." He'd have to take her with him. No matter what she promised and no matter how sincerely she apologized, he couldn't leave her alone in his house.

But it would also be fun. He loved the snowmobile and this was perfect weather for it. He'd take her out and show her the ranch—a perfect, pristine white version of his ranch, that was—and then he'd take her over to where there were some wild holly bushes. They'd need to get a tree, so he'd better pack a rope and…

It had been thirteen years since he'd almost asked Cindy to marry him. It'd been four years since his parents started going south for the winter, testing out retirement and avoiding things like blizzards and Beaumonts.

He was startled to realize that this was the first time he'd had company for Christmas in his adult life. But that wasn't as startling as it was to realize how much he had missed having someone to talk to. Yeah, he talked to his parents, but this was different.

She leaned into him, shoulder to shoulder. "You know, I don't think I've taken a day off in… Well, can't remember when. This has been—okay, maybe not a vacation," she said with a rueful smile. "This has been nice."

"Better than being miserable," he agreed. "We'll have fun tomorrow."

She didn't pull away from him. Instead, they

stood next to each other, watching the moonlight sparkle over the landscape.

It was so tempting to think that the rest of the world didn't exist anymore. She wasn't a television personality and he wasn't going to have to walk into town dressed as Santa Claus in less than three days and wonder if everyone looked at him and saw a Beaumont instead of a Wesley. Right now, it was just him and her, the quiet and the snow.

He was struck with the oddest urge to keep it this way. He wanted to stay in the present. This time was a gift, in its own way, and he wanted to make the most of it.

Without really making a conscious choice, he slid his arm around her shoulders and hugged her tight. "If I get the generator going tomorrow, we can watch movies. What's your favorite Christmas movie?"

Unexpectedly, it took her a long time to answer. "I've never really celebrated like this before. I tend to skip Christmas. For obvious reasons," she added with a sigh.

Not for the first time, he wondered about what she had said about herself—a whiny, spoiled brat who ruined everything. There was a certain measure of truth to the fact that she had upset his life—but he wouldn't go so far as to say that she'd ruined it.

It wasn't the sort of thing a person said about herself. It was, however, the sort of thing someone might say to a little girl, and that little girl might believe it.

"We've got time," he said, giving her a squeeze. She rested her head on his chest. "We can watch as many as you want."

Another shiver passed through her. "Hot cocoa?" he asked. He didn't understand his strange urge to take care of her but he was tired of fighting against it. He would regret it...eventually. But right now? He was just going to go with it.

She looked up at him, her eyes wide and sparkling with humor. "Only if you have marshmallows."

"What kind of man do you take me for? Of course I have marshmallows."

Together, they turned toward the kitchen. He didn't let go of her and she didn't pull away from him and that was okay. The more time he spent with her, the harder it was to see the morning television host who traded in gossip and innuendo.

Instead, she was just a woman. Natalie. Complicated and messy—yes. No one here would argue with that.

But, when she wasn't trying to be a morning television host, she was also soft and vulnerable, the kind of woman who could find happiness in marshmallows.

He was being an idiot. This was nothing more than a delusion. A pleasant one, but a delusion all the same. There was no guarantee that anything they said or did wouldn't wind up on her show.

But he hadn't expected this feeling of freedom.

She already knew the truth. He didn't have to keep hiding it from her. He could just be himself. Well, maybe not entirely himself.

What a mess.

In the kitchen, he got out the Ovaltine and the marshmallows while she put the kettle back on. "Ovaltine?" she asked, not even bothering to hide her amusement. "You're really just a big kid, aren't you?"

He dug around in the pantry until he came up with the bottle of peppermint schnapps. "I didn't drink it spiked when I was a kid."

Her eyes widened and she stared at him and he remembered last night, when she'd made a move. Was she thinking about that again? Because he was. He'd been trying not to think about the way her body melted into his last night, the way her fingers had felt stroking over his cheek—but he'd been failing most of the day.

Would she try again? Would she press her breasts against his chest and run her fingers through his hair? Until he had no choice but to kiss her, long and hard and deep?

The more important question was, would he let her? Was he so hard up that he would ignore all logic and common sense and let himself get lost in her body?

He would. His gaze dropped to her mouth and she ran her tongue over her lower lip and he knew that, without reservation, he wouldn't be strong enough to push her away.

They doctored up their cocoa and carried it into the living room. "Here," he said, handing her his mug as he threw a few more logs on the fire. When he turned back around, she was sitting in the middle of the couch, watching him with those eyes of hers.

If he were smart, he'd get his mug back and sit on the floor. He'd maintain a modicum of distance between them.

But he must not be as smart as he thought he was because instead, he sat down next to her and put his arm around her, drawing her close. She gave him his mug and rested her head on his shoulder. In a comfortable silence, they sipped their cocoa and watched the flames dance.

"What would you be doing if I weren't here?" she asked.

"This. Except alone."

"You really don't have anyone?"

He took a long swig of his cocoa, letting the schnapps burn on its way down. "I have my parents, but it's not the same. They're snowbirds now and I won't see them until March."

"I haven't talked to my dad since last Christmas," she admitted. "I try once a year but...it's not worth it."

"It must be rough during the holidays."

She shrugged and burrowed deeper against his

chest. He rested his head on the top of hers. Everything about this was a mistake but, God help him, he wasn't going to get off this couch anytime soon. "I stay busy. Really, Christmas is just another day."

That was possibly the saddest thing she had said yet. "Christmas is one of the best days of the year— and I'll prove it to you. Assuming we can get out, I'm supposed to be Santa in two days at the Christmas Eve party in Firestone. And you," he said, giving her a tight squeeze, "are going to be Santa's little helper."

Which was yet another piece of evidence that he had lost his mind. If he could get her to Firestone, someone was supposed to come get her. He didn't know who but that wasn't his problem. He would get her to town, someone would retrieve her and at some point when he could plow out his drive, he would get her car back to her. That had been the plan.

But it wasn't the plan anymore. He had to show her that Christmas was more than just another day. It was a time of hope and renewal. It was a time of change.

And since everything had already changed and would continue to change, he might as well spread the joy around and hope for the best.

Deep in the back of his mind, he knew his days of anonymity were numbered. She asked too many questions—questions other people would keep asking. But maybe he could…

Hell, he didn't know. Maybe he could get out in

front of it? But he wasn't even sure how to do that. He could contact Zeb Richards. Or even Chadwick Beaumont. They were both his half brothers. CJ had to let them know what was coming and maybe they'd have the public relations know-how to spin the impact in a positive direction for everyone involved.

Natalie looked up at him. "You'd let me help you hand out presents?"

"It's better to give than receive. It restores your faith in humanity."

She looked at him for a long time, as if she couldn't believe what she was seeing. He felt the same way. Away from cameras and relatives and townsfolk, he was starting to realize that Natalie Baker was someone he could like quite a bit.

She nuzzled back into his side. "Do you ever talk to them?"

He didn't have to ask who *them* were. "No."

"When Zeb Richards got married, we all wondered if you would show up. Everyone was there."

He knew. That wedding had been the focus of weeks worth of coverage on *A Good Morning with Natalie Baker.* "I saw."

He had gotten an email inviting him, but he hadn't wanted to go public. Months ago, Zeb had contacted him and asked him to come to dinner. Looking back, CJ now knew that was the beginning of the end. Zeb had found him and their other illegitimate half brother, Daniel, and like an older brother, Zeb had invited both of them to join him at the Beaumont Brewery as they took it back.

But CJ wasn't interested in Zeb's version of revenge. Beaumonts weren't to be trusted, so he had walked away.

He remembered something now. Zeb had given a press conference where he'd talked about the brewery being back in Beaumont hands. Natalie had covered it. In fact, she had been the one to get the final piece of information out of Zeb that no one else had—that there was a third bastard out there somewhere.

She was nothing if not tenacious.

"What will you do, now that you know?" He would have to face whatever was coming head-on— but he didn't want this to be a runaway train that plowed him down.

"My ratings are slipping. My job is on the line and I don't know how to do anything else," she told him in a small voice. "I told my producer I would find you and if I don't, he'll pull me off the air." He could feel her curling into a ball, getting smaller. He drank the rest of his cocoa, set his cup to the side and wrapped both arms around her. "I don't know what I am if I'm not Natalie Baker."

He lifted her up and settled her onto his lap. He shouldn't want to comfort her because she was going to ruin everything. No, that wasn't right. She was going to *change* everything and that was a different thing entirely.

But, as he ran his hand up and down her back, he wondered if maybe it wasn't time for a change.

"I still don't want to be your headline. I'm not some celebrity you can package and resell. This is my life. I'm Bell and Pat Wesley's son."

"You're a good man, CJ." Which was no kind of answer. She wrapped her arms around his waist and held on and CJ thought maybe he didn't really need an answer. Not right now.

"I think you're a good woman, too. When you're not trying so hard to be someone else."

They sat there for a long time. CJ's eyes grew heavy as the fire mesmerized him and the warmth of her body sank deep into his bones.

Just as he was about to slip off to sleep, he thought he heard her whisper, "No, I'm not."

Seven

"Natalie."

Natalie moaned, burrowing deeper into the warmth that surrounded her. Was it bright out? It seemed bright. She squeezed her eyes closed even tighter. She didn't want to wake up.

"Natalie," the voice repeated again. This time, she was aware that the voice was low and very close to her ear.

CJ. That was his voice. And those arms around her waist? Those were CJ's arms. He was warm and comfortable and safe and she didn't ever want to get up.

Wait a minute. CJ's arms were around her? And

that warm, solid chest she was nestling against—that was CJ's chest?

Oh, hell. What had she done? She tried to think. Had they had sex? She couldn't recall. And that seemed a shame because if she were going to have sex with CJ, she wanted to remember it.

Something stroked over her forehead. "Why are you frowning?" And then something else touched her right where she undoubtedly had a divot. Something warm but wet.

His lips.

Oh, *hell*.

"I hate to wake you, but we need to get up," he said gently, his lips moving against her skin.

Without moving, she tried to take stock. Her cheek was pressed against a sweater and her hand was resting on the same. Slowly, she wiggled her toes—her socks were still on. Were they fully clothed?

She bit the bullet. "Is there any way to make this not awkward?"

"Why would this be awkward?"

At that, she cracked open an eye and stared up at him. He leaned back enough that he could look at her—but there was very little space between them. She realized her head was resting on his arm and his hand was stroking her hair. "Last night, we…"

"Yes?"

Her cheeks began to heat. "What did we do?"

This close, that half smile was even more dangerous because all she would have to do to taste it would be to tilt his head down and press her lips against his. "We had cocoa in front of the fire. I might have been a little heavy with the peppermint schnapps, because we fell asleep."

Now she had both eyes open. She could see the distinctive flecks of green and brown in his. At a distance, they were hazel. But this close? She could see the two different parts that made one whole. "And that's it?"

It was his turn to wrinkle his brow. "Yeah."

She couldn't believe it. This had to be a first. Any other time she had been incapacitated and alone with a man, she'd woken up in various states of undress and she never could remember if she'd said yes or no. It hadn't mattered anyway. When she woke up with a man's arms around her and the taste of him in her mouth, it'd always been proof that someone had wanted her and that was the most important thing. More important than the hollow feeling she always had as she pulled on her clothes and did the walk of shame.

CJ was out-and-out frowning at her now. "I think you hang out with the wrong kind of people." That was all he said about it, but it was enough. He understood what she hadn't said.

She couldn't look at him and see confusion and maybe a little bit of anger. So she buried her face against his chest. "Do we have to get up?"

"Only if you want heat and hot water," he teased. "It's going to be a beautiful day. We could actually leave the living room."

She took the change of topic and ran with it. "Even the kitchen, too?"

He chuckled. The sound came straight out of his chest and surrounded her. "You crazy dreamer, you. Come on," he said more insistently. "I have big plans for you today and tomorrow's Christmas Eve." With that, he leaned down and gave her a firm kiss on the forehead. But before she could kiss him back he forcibly sat her upright and all but rolled her off the couch. "Get moving!"

He was just too damn decent. It wasn't healthy and it wasn't normal, she thought as she splashed cold water on her face in the bathroom. Anyone else would have pressed their advantage. She'd already come on to him once. She liked him. He was gorgeous as sin—but not a sinner. If he started kissing her, she wouldn't have stopped him, regardless of how tipsy she might or might not have been.

But it also seemed as if maybe he liked her, too. He hadn't at first—that much had been obvious. But the longer they were trapped in this house together, the more relaxed he became. The more comfortable he became, the more he touched her—but not in a pushy way. She remembered the feeling of his arm around her shoulders as they stared out at the moon-lit snowscape and how easy it had been curling up next to him and sipping the spiked hot chocolate on the couch. It had been warm and comfortable and safe. She hadn't had to be someone else to keep his interest.

And now he had big plans for her, and tomorrow night if they could make it to town on a snowmobile, he was going to be Santa for some sort of town party.

Did she want to stay for this party? Because originally, he'd wanted someone to pick her up in town and take her far, far away. She wouldn't get her car until the road was clear and she had no idea when that was going to happen.

But who was going to come get her? Steve, her producer? Kevin? He would rather see her freeze to death so he could have her time slot. She doubted that a car service would come this far north to fetch her.

The fact was, she had nowhere to go and no one waiting for her. The second fact was that the sooner she went back to Denver, back to her sleek apartment with black furniture and white walls and white carpeting—and not a single Christmas decoration in sight—the sooner she would be faced with another Christmas alone. She'd have to psych herself up to make her annual call to her father to wish him a merry Christmas and hope against hope that this time, he'd do the same.

And the sooner she would have to face Steve and make some sort of decision about the third lost Beaumont bastard.

Could she really do that to CJ? Could she drag him kicking and screaming into the public eye and subject him to the same sort of trolling that she dealt with every day? He didn't deserve it and he didn't want it. He was too good of a man to throw to the wolves because he wouldn't defend himself. He was too damn polite to survive in her world. She knew it and she thought he knew it, too.

She couldn't hide out here forever, though— tempting as the idea was. She had obligations and sooner or later, she was going to have to decide.

Was CJ her story? Or was he something else?

Later, she decided. She would choose later.

By the time she got out of the bathroom, CJ had grown three whole sizes. He was wearing a full-body snowsuit thing with a hood that made him look like a tan Abominable Snowman. "Good heavens. I suppose that crime against fashion is warm?"

He laughed. "You're more than welcome to brave the snow in that cute little coat of yours." He held out another snowsuit.

With an exaggerated sigh, she took it from him. "After you went to all that trouble to keep me from freezing to death once, I'd hate to undo your hard work." The suit weighed a ton in her arms. "Good heavens," she repeated, lugging the whole thing over to the couch.

"It's about sixteen degrees outside. I don't want

you to freeze," he said. "Then I'd have to warm you up again."

Her head shot up. It wasn't so much what he said but the way he said it. The low timbre to his voice made her feel things in places hidden by far more than a snowsuit.

"I didn't think there was any hot water left," she said carefully.

"There are other ways to warm a body up."

Heat flooded her as she stared up at him. He shouldn't be that sexy—not in that hideous snowsuit. But the way he looked at her, like he wanted to unwrap her for Christmas…

She let her gaze drift over his body—the body that had been in her arms just a few short minutes ago. "Like how?"

Because maybe she wanted to be unwrapped. Maybe she wanted him to peel every single one of the seven thousand layers of clothing off and lay her out in front of that fire. The only thing that was missing was a tree dripping in lights—but she could be his present and he could be hers. Outside of the white-elephant exchange at work every year, she hadn't had a present to unwrap in…well, in a very long time.

The muscle in his jaw twitched. "Shoveling snow will keep you plenty warm."

"Oh." She cleared her throat and focused on shoving her legs into the massive snowsuit. "Is that what we're doing?"

"For starters. The snowmobile can go up to forty miles an hour. That's a wind chill you don't mess around with."

He held out something that looked like a stocking cap, but when Natalie took it, she felt neoprene instead. "I didn't realize we were going to be robbing banks today," she joked as she yanked it down over her hair.

"With a face like yours, you could get away with robbing banks." As he said it, CJ stepped into her. He tucked a few loose strands under the mask and tugged it down until it was in the right position. "No one would think someone as beautiful as you would be capable of it. They'd be falling all over themselves to give you money."

It didn't seem possible, but he was entirely serious. His gaze was fastened on hers as his fingers stroked over the few inches of exposed skin on her cheeks. Then he was pulling the hood of the snowsuit over her ski mask and wrapping a scarf around the whole thing. "There," he said with satisfaction as he stepped back to look at her. "You probably can't put your arms down."

Natalie gave it a try and discovered she could—but only a little. She was beginning to sweat. She could safely say she had never had on this many layers before and she had lived almost her entire life in Denver. She wanted to go outside and see how weatherproof she was, but at the same time, she couldn't quite pull herself away from CJ's gaze.

"Is there something wrong?" It was hard not to feel insecure about her looks when there was only a third of her face showing. No doubt, she looked lumpy and bumpy and the exact opposite of glamorous.

The way CJ was looking at her, though… There was a light in his eyes that hadn't been there yesterday and she didn't think it was solely due to the sunlight flooding the big house. "Nope," he said, turning away and pulling his own ski mask over his head. "Let's go see how bad it is."

It was pretty bad. They had to go out the front door because there was a five-foot-tall drift blocking the kitchen door. Even then, they still had to shovel their way off of the porch. Walking through this much snow was, hands down, the most intense cardio workout Natalie had ever had. It was like slogging through mud, only colder. If she hadn't had CJ by her side, she might've panicked because how the hell was she ever going to leave? Even if she wasn't sure she wanted to leave, she would have to go home at one point or another. But her car was nothing but a lump in the snow and the cold was so biting she could feel it slipping under the neoprene face mask.

She could be out here until spring. And the thing was, she had no idea if that thought terrified her or not.

She didn't have time to figure it out, either, because all of a sudden, a snowball hit her in the arm. She whipped her head around to see CJ in the process of patting another ball of snow into a sphere.

"Oh, no, you don't," she yelled, dropping her shovel and scooping up snow. She launched it at him before she even got it into a ball. It hit him in the chest and disintegrated with a *pfft*.

"Hey," he hollered—but he was laughing.

They lobbed snowballs at each other—Natalie missed more often than not, but CJ had a good arm. Of course he did. He'd probably been having snowball fights and playing catch in the backyard with his dad for years. She hadn't. She never even had a house with a yard. There was something so sweet about a snowball fight—sweeter still, that CJ went to great efforts not to hit her in the face.

She was having fun. Honest-to-goodness fun. It was such a foreign concept she almost didn't recognize it. Laughing, they made their way back to the side of the house, where CJ called a truce.

The generator was housed in a small shed less than five feet from the back door. For a moment, Natalie felt guilty. If he hadn't had to drag her woefully unprepared behind into his house and keep her from freezing to death, he would've been able to get the generator started already. But once the storm had hit, there was no getting out here.

"Can you work on digging out the back door while I get into the shed?" CJ asked cautiously, as if he didn't believe she knew how to move snow from one place to another.

"Sure." The air bit at her lungs and her nose was probably going to be permanently red after this, but beyond that, she was plenty warm. She had to trudge back and grab her shovel from where she had dropped it during the snowball fight. Then she got to work.

She did spinning classes and Zumba and she ran—but nothing prepared her for shoveling five feet of snow. It was an intensive, full-body workout because the snow was a little wet. Which was good for snowballs, but made for heavy shoveling. Finally, she got the door cleared and then began working on meeting up where CJ had dug out the shed. He'd already disappeared inside of it and in a few minutes, she heard a whirring sound.

She knew she should be thrilled that the power was back on. She could use a hot shower like nobody's business. But that also meant that, if she and CJ didn't have to stay in front of the fireplace for warmth, they could sleep in separate bedrooms. They wouldn't have a good excuse to sit in front of the fire and lean against each other and drink spiked cocoa. They could go back to being more like themselves.

The thought saddened her. But then she remembered that he had promised her Christmas movies once they got their chores done today.

CJ emerged from the little shed and whistled in

approval. "Great job. You ready to get to the barn? I need to feed my horses. They're probably starved. Then we can get the snowmobile out."

Natalie nodded and they began trudging the hundred feet to the barn. The barn was cold, but not freezing. CJ showed her where the grain was and told her how many scoops to put in each bucket. The horses pawed at the doors and CJ spoke to them in low, steady voices.

"It's going to be a while, boys," he told them as he carried hay and filled water buckets. He didn't even make fun of her when she jumped as one horse sniffed at her. "You ever been around horses before?"

"No—I suppose that's obvious. I really am just a city girl."

He could've made her feel stupid for not knowing what to do—but he didn't. Instead, he gave her a reassuring grin and said, "You're doing a great job." And again, that was one of those things that could've been a load of bull—but coming from him, seemed one hundred percent sincere.

They worked in the barn for almost an hour. CJ had six different horses and he spent time with each one of them. He clearly cared for his animals, which just confirmed that this was who he was as a person. He wasn't acting all nice to her just because he wanted something from her. He simply *was* this nice.

Again, guilt pinched her. Because if she made

him her story to save her job, all this would change for him.

She tried to tell herself that it wouldn't last forever, him being a hot news item. Sure, he might be in for a long winter, but sooner or later, something would happen and CJ would no longer be the focus of the public's attention. Perhaps someone would know something about Daniel Lee and there was always the upcoming birth of Zeb Richards's baby to look forward to. Or one of the younger legitimate Beaumonts could do something crazy. *Something* would happen, she told herself, and CJ would fade away from the public's awareness. Her ratings would be secure and her show would be safe.

And after that...

"Ready?" CJ asked. At some point, he had pushed his hood and ski mask down. Even bundled up like a snowman, he was too handsome.

"Yes." She had to be.

At the far end of the barn was a bigger door and next to that, a room where three different snowmobiles sat. It took some work, but CJ got the biggest one out of the barn and up onto the top of the snow. It was unfortunate that he was wearing just as many layers as she was because she would've loved to have seen all those muscles in action.

Maybe this summer, she thought. But even as the thought occurred to her, she pushed it aside. She wouldn't be back. CJ wouldn't want her out here.

This time, just the two of them, was a special time. Once they went back to their separate rooms, their separate lives, the magic of the moment would be shattered and they'd never get it back again.

She'd never wake up in his arms again, warm and comfy. She'd never go to sleep with him again, either—knowing that she could trust him completely.

God, what was wrong with her? She didn't want these melancholy thoughts. She didn't want the sensation of guilt. She didn't want to know that something was wrong and have to do it anyway. But she couldn't see another way to save the life she'd made for herself.

She ruined everything, after all.

"Here we go," CJ said, infectious enthusiasm in his voice. Even though she was conflicted about what she wanted to happen with him, she smiled as he helped her up onto the back of the snowmobile and took his place in front. "Now you hang on real tight," he said before he gunned the engine.

Natalie just had time to get her arms around his waist when the snowmobile lurched forward, picked up speed and then began to fly. She buried her face against his back to protect the exposed skin but even then, she couldn't resist peeking out as the pure white landscape zipped by them.

The snowmobile was much louder than she had anticipated and she wished it could've been quiet so she could have heard the wilderness around them. As they went past, birds skittered out of trees and she thought she saw a rabbit or two ducking for cover. But this wasn't that different from them being in the living room. They were alone in this pristine world and Natalie liked it far more than she should.

He slowed and pointed to dark moving shapes in the distance. "My herd," he shouted back at her.

"Do we need to feed them?" she yelled, remembering how hungry the horses had been.

He shook his head. "I laid out extra hay. They'll have to dig for it, though. But they'll be all right."

Then they roared on for a while until suddenly, CJ eased to a stop in front of some snow-covered lumps. "Here," he said loudly—Natalie's ears were ringing from the ride.

"Here what?" As far she could tell, they were in the middle of nowhere. But she slid off the snowmobile and waited.

CJ trudged over to the lumps. He kicked at them until the snow went flying. Natalie gasped. The deep green leaves and bright red berries stood out against the white snow. "Holly?"

CJ nodded and produced a knife from somewhere. He cut off several large branches and gave them to her to hold. Then he trudged a little farther back to a slightly larger looking lump. Again, he knocked off more snow, revealing some evergreens. He cut long boughs and handed them to Natalie as well. "One more thing," he said, motioning for her to set the foliage down on the back of the snowmobile. Then he held out his hand and she took it.

Together, they trudged deeper into the woods. The snow hadn't drifted as high under the cover of the trees. Instead of being indistinguishable lumps of white, the shrubs and trees were instead dusted with a thick coating of snow. She stopped as a pair of cardinals settled onto a branch of a nearby pine tree like two ornaments hung just so.

CJ followed her gaze and saw the birds. He took a step back so their shoulders were touching again and let her watch for a few minutes as the birds hopped from limb to snow-covered limb. Nature had decorated the tree for them. It was the most perfect thing she'd ever seen.

When the birds finally fluttered off, Natalie turned to CJ and said, "I never knew it could be this beautiful."

He stared down at her, a mysterious smile on his face. "Neither did I."

She didn't think he was talking about the birds. She dropped her gaze, embarrassed. Then CJ took her hand again. They moved on a little farther until he stopped and pointed at a cute little tree. "What do you think?"

"It's lovely." And it was. About six feet tall, the little pine tree had a nearly perfect cone shape and thick branches covered in snow.

"Then it's yours." She was surprised when CJ produced a small saw out of a different pocket.

"Really?"

"It *is* Christmas," he said, getting down on his hands and knees and sawing through the trunk. "And what's Christmas without a tree?"

A mix of strange emotions fluttered through her. She couldn't remember the last time she'd had a Christmas tree—just that one in that picture, when they were still a happy family.

But CJ was going to give her real tree—a real Christmas. One she could remember.

When the tree fell to the ground, he stood up and looked at her. "Are you crying?"

Natalie sniffed, swiping at her eyes with the back of her thick work gloves. "No," she lied and she didn't even care if he saw her tell.

CJ looked at her for a moment longer. "Good," he said in that gentle voice of his. "I wouldn't want your face to freeze on the way back."

She didn't want that, either. "How are we going to get the tree back? I can't hold it and hold on to you, too."

He cocked an eyebrow at her and grabbed the trunk of the tree. "I have my ways," he promised. Slowly they began walking toward the snowmobile.

Once they made it back, he produced some rope from yet another mysterious pocket. In short order, CJ had tied the tree onto the back of the snowmobile.

He had enough rope left over to bundle the boughs of holly and pine together. Natalie tucked the bundle under one arm and with the other she held tight to his waist. Then they were screaming across the countryside toward his home.

When they got back into the house, it was noticeably warmer. She struggled to get the thick gloves off her hands and the hood off her head. "I'd hate to see it really cold out here," she mumbled, trying to kick off a boot.

The next thing she knew, CJ was in front of her. "Here," he said in that husky voice of his. He held her by the shoulders and made her stand up straight. "Are you too cold?"

Her face, her hands, her feet—yes. But other parts of her?

CJ pushed down the hood and pulled the mask over her head. The rush of air around the back of her neck made her shiver. "A little," she said, but anything else she wanted to add died on her tongue when he reached up and began to pull the zipper of her suit.

He was unwrapping her. *Slowly. Oh, yeah*—some parts of her were beginning to burn. She wanted to shift her feet to take some of the pressure off of her center, but she didn't want to break the spell.

"You never did tell me the other way of warming someone up." She was surprised to hear her own voice come out sultry.

Because she wanted this. Not the story, not her

ratings—the man. She wanted CJ selfishly, all for herself. She didn't want to share him.

He pushed the snowsuit down her shoulders and then he stepped even closer, skimming his hands over her waist and her hips, shoving the warm, heavy suit down her legs. "If someone is too cold," he said as his hands kept right on skimming. He fell to his knees and lifted her left leg up. "Then the best way to warm them up is with body heat."

She'd seen enough movies to know what he was talking about—two people with as little clothing as possible tucked under blankets.

She swallowed and said in her most innocent voice, "How do you do that?"

But he didn't see her tell because he was pulling the suit off of one foot and then the other. Then, slowly, he climbed to his feet. His pupils were so black she almost couldn't see the brown or the green in his eyes and he was breathing hard. But he didn't say anything. He just stared at her.

She couldn't take it. She reached for his zipper and said, "Maybe you should show me."

But before she could get him unwrapped, he grabbed her hands. "The water heater should have caught up by now. You go first."

She bit back the disappointment. What was wrong? She wanted him. He wanted her. The last few days had been as close to perfect as she was capable of imagining. So why wasn't he giving in?

Then a new thought occurred to her. The shower she'd been in had been more than big enough for two people. Water and soap and hands everywhere—that would warm her up. Hell, just thinking about it was making her hot. "You could join—"

He cut her off. "I'll get the tree set up," he said as he turned away. "Go on." It was not a request. It was an order.

She opened her mouth to ask what she'd done wrong. Why didn't he want her? Was it just because of her morning show or was it something else?

That insidious voice in the back of her head whispered, *Of course he doesn't want you. No one does.*

But she didn't want to listen to that voice. Not today, when things had been so perfect and there was the promise of decorating Christmas trees and movies and…something more. Something wonderful.

"Go on," CJ repeated, motioning with his chin toward the stairs.

She didn't answer for a long, long moment—but finally, common sense won out. "Thanks. A shower would be perfect right now." It was only after she said it that she saw he was staring at her throat.

Crap.

Eight

For the second time in three days, CJ was forcing himself not to think about Natalie Baker naked in his shower. And if he thought it had gone poorly the first time, it was an absolute flipping disaster today.

Because the woman in his shower today seemed like a completely different woman from the one he'd dragged into this house a few days ago. Instead of belligerent and cocky and hell-bent on using her beautiful body as a weapon, the Natalie he'd come to know was someone else entirely. Soft and vulnerable and easy to be around. Someone who didn't mind shoveling a lot of snow and could see the beauty in a pair of songbirds in a tree.

It could still be a trick, he told himself as he dug

out the tree stand and got the tree set up. All of this sweetness could be part of her larger plan to weasel information out of him.

That's not what his gut told him, though, and up until this point in his life, his gut had been a fairly reliable indicator of who to trust and who to avoid.

And what was he thinking? Unzipping her snow-suit for her? Peeling it off of her body like he had a right to touch her? Because he didn't. He *couldn't.*

Okay, when she looked up at him with those beautiful blue eyes like he was this rare specimen just because he did something any decent man would do—yeah, that hit him midchest. And, sure, when he'd woken up this morning with her body curling into his, all warm and soft and sleepy, it'd hit him in other places.

He shouldn't have kissed her on the forehead this morning. He shouldn't have helped her out of her things this afternoon. And at no point did discussing getting naked and under the covers for "warmth" become a good idea.

Because that's what she was right now. Naked. In the guest room. In the shower. Hot water sluicing over her bare back, her breasts, as she ran the soap over the pointed tips—

He cleared his throat and adjusted his pants. He had crap to do. He had to focus. There was the coming revelation that he was the third Beaumont bastard heir. There was the Firestone Christmas party tomorrow night. There was a tree that needed tinsel, dammit.

He would have to call Zeb, he decided as he headed down to the basement—without a flashlight this time—and grabbed one of the bins of ornaments. The man owed him a favor. After all, it was Zeb's fault that anyone knew about CJ in the first place. The least his half brother could do was offer some sort of PR backup. CJ would call Zeb and somehow get Natalie back to Denver. And after that…

After that, it was back to a long, cold, dark winter out on the ranch. He'd tend to his horses and try to keep his cattle from freezing to death and watch a lot of movies and drink a lot of beer.

Alone. His thoughts drifted back upstairs, where Natalie was no doubt drying off and putting on fresh clothes. Was it selfish of him to wish that she could stay here for a little while longer? Maybe through the New Year? He might be able to plow the drive, but towing her car out of that drift without ripping the axle off of it would be next to impossible without a major warm-up. And she wouldn't want to leave without her car, right?

She could stay, he decided. It really wouldn't be that bad. He could help her get more comfortable around the horses, show her other parts of the ranch—tomorrow, he really did have to go check on the cattle. And then, after they'd done the day's chores, they could…

He dropped his head and jammed his hands onto his hips. He didn't want the images—Natalie in his arms, naked and bare to him. He wanted to stroke his fingers over her skin and see how her body reacted. Would her nipples tighten with his touch? What kind of noises would she make if he touched her?

This whole day had been an exercise in painful lust. It wasn't right that a woman could make a snowsuit and ski mask look sexy, but she did. Standing out there in the woods this afternoon, watching that pair of cardinals coo and sing to each other— she had been the most beautiful woman he had ever seen. And the look on her face when he cut down the Christmas tree for her?

She pulled at something in him and it was getting harder and harder to resist.

First things first. Tomorrow night was Christmas Eve and he was pretty sure that, barring another weather disaster, he would be able to make the trek into Firestone for the annual Christmas party. While she was still upstairs, he made his phone calls. Everything was still a go—it might be a lot of horse-drawn sleighs and snowmobiles, but they were going to have a parade for the kids, come hell or high water.

Then, quickly, he left a message for Zeb and Daniel. "Natalie Baker has found me. I'm not sure what she's going to do. I'm trying to convince her that I'm not a story, but just in case, be ready." He wished he could tell them what to be ready for, specifically, but he had no idea.

Then, knowing he was running out of time, he pulled her phone out of his back pocket. He'd kept it with him at all times for the last several days. It was tempting to turn it on—almost too tempting. She had said that no one would miss her for Christmas and he wasn't sure if he believed that. If he turned on her phone, would there be notifications from someone who was thinking of her? A father, a boyfriend—any friend? Or would it be more of those horrible tweets and notifications? No one should have to put up with that.

That was what he was afraid of, he realized. It wasn't just that people would know who he was—it was that they would treat him like they treated her.

He didn't turn on her phone. He didn't want to let those trolls into his house in any way, shape or form. Instead, he slid her phone back into his pocket just as he heard her footsteps coming down the stairs.

What he saw took his breath away and he couldn't even say why. She was wearing another pair of jeans with a shirt and a sweater over it, plus thick socks. There shouldn't be anything sensual about her—but there was. It was all in her face, he realized. The way she looked at him did some mighty funny things to him. The tingling started low in his back and raced along his limbs until the only thing that would soothe it would be to pull her into his arms, just like she'd been when he woke up this morning.

"Hi," she said almost shyly.

Her gaze met his. There was something about her that glowed—something that hadn't been there the first time he'd seen her in the feed store. She didn't have that glow when she was on television. It was so hard to even see that woman when he looked at the Natalie standing before him. It didn't seem possible that they were the same person.

"Better?"

She dropped her chin and looked up at him through thick lashes. "I'm still a little chilly." As if to demonstrate this, she wrapped her arms around her waist and gave a comical little shiver.

He knew what that meant—that was an invitation. If he walked over and put his arms around her shoulders and pulled her against him, she would go willingly. Happily, even. There was a big part of him that wanted to do exactly that. He knew he had reasons why he shouldn't—although those reasons were getting harder to remember all the time.

"Come stand in front of the fire."

She notched an eyebrow at him, as if she were disappointed he hadn't taken her up on the challenge. But she did as he asked. Or started to, anyway. Because when she looked past him, she saw the tree and her whole face lit up.

"Oh," she breathed, her eyes wide with surprise and joy. "It's the most beautiful thing I've ever seen."

"Wait until we decorate it," he told her. Would it be so wrong if he kissed her? Would it be such a terrible thing if he let himself pretend, even for a little while, that reality wasn't waiting for them once the snow melted?

Could he trust her to kiss and not tell? Could he trust himself with keeping it to just a kiss?

She turned to him, her eyes luminous. He didn't think he could and he wasn't sure he wanted to. He'd kept himself apart from everyone but his family for so long that he had forgotten what it felt like to have a connection with another person. But he felt that now.

"Do we have to decorate it?" she asked. "It's so pretty just the way it is."

He couldn't help himself. He stepped in close and stroked her cheek with the back of his hand. "It is, isn't it?" But he wasn't looking at the tree when he said it.

She held his hand against her face. "You're still cold," she said, her voice barely above a whisper.

Was he? Because he didn't feel cold. All he could feel was the warmth of her skin against his. "I don't mind."

Unexpectedly, a shadow crossed her face. "Oh," she said with disappointment. Then she stepped away and looked back at the tree. "I understand."

"Understand what?" Because he hadn't meant

anything by that—at least, nothing to make her shut down on him.

She walked over to the bins of ornaments and popped the lid off one. "It's fine," she said in a voice that made it clear it was anything but.

"Natalie," he said, keeping his voice steady. "What's fine?"

She stilled. "You don't want to take a shower and leave me alone in your house. Which is fine. I mean, I wouldn't violate your privacy—but I understand that you don't want to take that risk." She pulled out a roll of colored beads. "Where would you like these?"

He stared at the back of her head. "Natalie," he said with more force this time.

She stood, but she didn't turn around. "Do you wrap these around the tree?"

He closed the distance between them and turned her around so she had no choice but to look at him. "Natalie, that's not what I meant."

She closed her eyes. "You don't owe me an explanation. I know this hasn't been how you wanted to spend your holiday and I—"

She didn't get any further than that because CJ kissed her. Roughly. Her eyes widened and she gave a little squeak that almost made him pull away. But before he could, her eyelids drifted shut as she sighed into his mouth. Her arms went around his neck and pulled him in close and then she was kissing him back. Her mouth opened and with a groan, CJ dipped his tongue into her.

God, she tasted so good—sweet and earthy, with a hint of vanilla. She was like a cookie and he wanted to nibble at her. Slowly.

But he couldn't. Dammit, he *couldn't*. There were reasons. Okay, so he couldn't exactly remember what those reasons were—not when she moaned into him like she was doing as his tongue dipped in and out of her mouth. But just because he couldn't remember them didn't mean there weren't any so, reluctantly, he forced himself to lean back. Her eyes were closed and her chest was heaving and he almost kissed her again right then and there. But then her eyelashes fluttered and she looked at him and there was a happiness to her that he hadn't expected to see. She was happy that he'd kissed her.

Doubt slithered in. Was she happy because she'd wanted him to kiss her? Or was this part of the story she was researching?

But then she touched his cheek and, with a crooked smile, said, "There. You're warmer already."

She turned to go, but CJ caught her in his arms and held her tight. "Natalie," he breathed against her skin but he didn't know what he was asking. Did he want her to kiss him? Did he want some sort of reassurance that this was real? Did he want something more?

He didn't know and it was only mildly reassuring that she didn't seem to know, either. He touched his forehead to hers but even that connection felt significant.

He hadn't had a serious relationship since college—since the last time he tried to tell someone that he was a Beaumont by birth.

The last time he had told someone about Hardwick Beaumont, it had ruined everything. But Natalie already knew about it. With each passing hour, it seemed to matter less, not more.

God, how he wanted it not to matter at all.

She was the one who broke the silence. "Go take a shower," she told him, a waver in her voice. "I won't decorate the tree without you."

He didn't want to ask this question but he asked it anyway. "What are you going to do?"

Her smile was a lot sadder. "It's been a long day. I'll probably just sit on the couch and watch the fire."

He could take her at her word because it *had* been a long day. He had gotten her up early and run her outside to shovel snow and then taken her on a ride on the snowmobile.

Or he could stay down here, forgo a shower and keep an eye on her.

He'd already kissed her. Hell, he had already made his choice. "I won't be long," he promised, stroking his fingers over her cheek. Her whole body shook with what he prayed was need.

God, he hoped he didn't regret this.

Nine

He had kissed her. *Hard.*

The kind of kiss that left a girl anxious and burning, that made sitting awkward and standing a misery. The kind of kiss that normally led to so much more than a full-body hug.

He had kissed her. And then left her alone.

Those two thoughts repeated over and over in her head as Natalie filled a coffee mug and curled up on the sofa. He had kissed her and left her alone in his house for the first time in days.

That was amazing enough. But what was even more amazing was the fact that she was doing exactly what she had told him she would. She was going to sit here and admire this beautiful tree that he had gotten for her and she was going to watch the fire dance and she was not going to pry into his life.

She didn't want him to be her story and she didn't want to share him or this time with anyone else. For someone who had lived so much of her life oversharing in an attempt to get people to look at her, it felt odd that she didn't want anyone else to know about this. But this time was hers and his. It didn't belong to anyone else.

So what was she supposed to do now? Keep hoping this semi-involuntary Christmas vacation would go on forever? That was no answer and she knew it. It was one thing to intrude on CJ's privacy and hospitality for a couple of days, but it was another thing to suggest that anything about this could become more permanent. Besides, she had a job to do—a job she loved.

At least, she *had* loved it.

Hadn't she?

She stared down at her coffee as if it held the answers. What if she hadn't loved her job? What if she actually hated it? What if putting herself on display and hoping to get noticed had secretly made her sick?

Because she was. Sick of the trolling and negativity. Sick of trying so hard to get a reaction that it stopped being about getting good reactions and started being about getting *any* reaction. She was sick of it all and she hadn't realized it until CJ had taken her phone away.

No, it was more than that. He had taken her phone away and then relentlessly treated her like a real human being. She wasn't a commodity or a collection of body parts. She was a woman and, after a kiss like that, she might even be a woman he could like. That wasn't a bad thing at all.

She didn't have relationships. So she had no idea if that were even a possibility.

She was so lost in thought that she didn't hear him come downstairs. One moment, she was contemplating what life would be like if she just…stopped. Stopped being the Natalie Baker of *A Good Morning with Natalie Baker*, stopped tweeting and sharing. Stopped trying to get everyone's attention and instead focused on keeping one man's attention.

The next moment, CJ was standing in front of her, smiling down at her as if he were relieved to find her exactly where she'd said she'd be. His hair was damp from the shower and she had the overwhelming urge to press a kiss to the base of his neck and see what he tasted like.

But she didn't. "Are we going to decorate the tree now?"

He looked so happy. This had been building for days now, this slow thaw. What would he be like if he melted completely?

"Let me put on some Christmas music and we'll get started."

Everything about this was new and exciting. She

only listened to Christmas music when she was on the air or in stores.

CJ loaded a streaming music mix, which meant they bopped from Elvis to Mariah Carey and then back to Bing Crosby. CJ knew the words to every single song and his singing voice wasn't half-bad.

They strung lights and beads and hung ornaments—some of which clearly went back to his childhood. But she didn't ask. It was enough to know that he'd had a wonderful childhood—because that much was obvious.

She thought of everything she knew about the Beaumont family—the divorces, the scandals, the rumors that people whispered. She knew a great deal about the Beaumonts—far more than was probably common knowledge. And she knew that a lot of them had not had happy childhoods. In that regard, she was more like his family than he was.

But he'd had a different life. One filled with homemade ornaments lovingly preserved and displayed every single year and Christmas carols and hot cocoa.

How would her life have been different if there'd been a little bit of hope at Christmas?

CJ was right, though—the tree undecorated was pretty, but the tree decorated? "It's stunning," she said as she felt an unexpected catch in the back of her throat.

Why hadn't she ever done this? She could've gotten a tree—even a small one, with twinkling lights and cute little ornaments that meant something to her, even if they didn't mean a single thing to anyone else. Why hadn't she celebrated Christmas before now?

Because Christmas was joy and happiness and fun. Christmas was hope and peace and she…

Did she deserve any of it?

"Christmas movies or football?" CJ asked, snapping her out of her thoughts.

She gave him a dull look, but couldn't keep the smile off of her face. "Movies," she said decisively. But then she added, "I haven't watched a lot of Christmas movies before, so you'll have to tell me what's good."

CJ popped a big bowl of popcorn and made more cocoa—he went a little lighter on the peppermint schnapps this time, but he still added some. Then they curled up on the couch and Natalie pulled the blanket over them and they started watching something called *A Christmas Story*.

"You've really never seen this before?" CJ asked as she giggled at the leg lamp.

She was trying so hard to seem normal—but clearly, she wasn't making it. Apparently, the whole world knew about the leg lamp. "I'm usually pretty busy during the holidays," she lied.

He stared at her for a long moment and she remembered that she had a tell. She was just about to say something else to cover her embarrassment when he said, "Well, I'm glad you were able to take some time off and hang out with me." Which was also not exactly the truth. "Surely you've seen some Christmas shows?"

She ignored the pity lacing the edge of that question. "Oh, yes—I remember *A Charlie Brown Christmas* and *Rudolph the Red-Nosed Reindeer* when I was a kid."

She remembered the feeling both shows had conveyed—of not belonging and wanting to so badly. And when she'd tried to watch the shows one long year after her mother had left, her dad had shattered the television screen with the remote.

How old had she been? Seven?

She pushed the unpleasant memories away and focused on the movie. And on CJ. His body was warm next to hers, and she once again found herself fighting the urge to press her breasts against his chest and kiss him. Not as thanks but because she wanted to.

And after that kiss earlier? Because he wanted her, too.

But she didn't. The kiss earlier had been damned near perfect and for the first time ever, she wondered if sex might make things…well, not worse. But more complicated. And she didn't want this to be complicated. She didn't want to kiss him and have him set her aside again.

She didn't want the rejection. And she really

didn't want that hollow feeling afterwards. If she and CJ had sex, she wanted it to mean something.

She wanted to mean something to him.

So it was better not to ask the question. Besides, there was a movie on. By the time it had ended, darkness had settled back over the living room. The popcorn bowl had been set aside and the empty mugs were somewhere on the floor. They had shifted so CJ was sprawled out on his back and Natalie was lying on his chest, the blanket pulled up over both of them. He was warm and solid—and since she was *not* imagining how warm and solid he'd be without his layers on—she was tempted to close her eyes and fall asleep in his arms. Because she knew that when she woke up, he'd be there and everything would be all right.

The temptation got a lot harder to avoid when he started stroking her hair. "Have you decided what you're going to do tomorrow?" he asked as he turned off the TV with the remote and wrapped his arm around her.

He was in no hurry to get up and that made her feel better. "I can try and see if someone can come get me in town tomorrow, if you want. But I've never had a Christmas like this," she told him truthfully.

He was silent for a long time but his hand still stroked over her hair. It should have been lulling her to sleep—but it wasn't. Every inch of her skin tingled with awareness. "It might be a while before your car gets out. And I don't know what the roads between here and Denver are like."

She curled her fingers into his sweater and lifted her chin up so she could look at him. His eyes were half-closed, but he was watching her. The hand that had been stroking her hair shifted so he was brushing a few stray strands away from her face and the other hand, which had been laying on her back, began to rub in circles that seemed to push her closer to him. Closer to his mouth. "And if I want to stay?"

"Because you want to go to the Christmas party tomorrow night?"

She shook her head.

She saw him swallow. "Because you're still gathering facts for your story?"

Just thinking about that made her want to cry. "No. This isn't about that."

He met her gaze with such strength that it made her quiver. What would it be like to have such conviction? "I don't want to be just a story to you."

"You're not," she promised, even as she wasn't entirely sure it was a promise she could keep.

He sighed and flopped his head back on the pillow, staring up at the ceiling. "But you need your story, don't you? And because my parents insisted on hiding the truth, now it's a thing. There's the small matter of the family fortune—and the family." His chest rose and fell with another heavy sigh. "I have brothers and sisters, but I don't want to give up my life to get them. Do you understand?"

She stared at him, trying to make sense of his words. Was he offering to—to what? Be interviewed? Even if he was, that didn't change the fact that he couldn't come out of obscurity without people noticing. That's not how this worked.

He was stuck—no way forward and no way back and she'd been the one to back him into this corner. But then he said, "I'm tired of hiding, Natalie."

She froze. What? She didn't have anything to do with him hiding. She wasn't the one keeping him out here, alone in the darkest part of winter.

Maybe she wasn't the only problem here. For some reason, the realization made her feel light-headed as she studied his face. Not a muscle clenched in his jaw. The man didn't know how to lie. Maybe…

"I'm tired of keeping other people's secrets," he went on. "I'm tired of lies. I don't want you to lie to me. Not anymore."

"I won't." Tentatively, she touched her fingertips to his cheek, above the line of his beard. This time, he didn't grab her hand and he didn't push her away. He let her stroke her fingers over his skin, exploring him.

It wasn't until she dragged her thumb over his lower lip—the same lip that had kissed her earlier—that he stopped her. "Natalie," he said as he stilled her hand—but even then, he didn't pull it away. Instead, he pressed a kiss to her palm. "Tell me what this is about," he pleaded. "Tell me the truth."

The truth. She couldn't give him much, but she could give him that. "You're a good man," she told him. "You're a kind, hard-working, damnably decent man and I like you." He was too good for her, but she liked him anyway.

She could use everything he'd said against him. She was pretty sure that, if she tried hard enough, she could convince herself she was doing him a favor, dragging him out of the shadows and into the bright spotlight that was always fixed on the Beaumont family. He didn't want to hide anymore? Well, she could fix that for him.

But that wouldn't be fair to him and the more time she spent with him, the less she could turn him into just a story. Just some ratings. Just...

Just something less than a man. A flesh-and-blood man who was studying her closely while he held her palm to his cheek.

She liked him far more than she should.

It might wind up costing her the one thing she'd always valued most of all: her job.

"I won't, CJ," she repeated, knowing this was right. God, everything about this was right. "You're more than a story to me."

This was the point where he should tell her not to touch him, tell her that he didn't trust her. At the very least, he should pull away and tell her to go to sleep.

He did none of those things. "If you stay," he said in a low, deep voice that did things to her, "I won't be able to keep myself from doing this."

His hands slid down to her bottom and pushed her up and she let him. She wanted him to. She braced her elbows on his chest and leaned into him and this time, she kissed *him*. He tasted like cocoa and peppermint—like Christmas. And all she wanted to do was drink him in and pretend, even if only for a little while, that she was good enough for him.

She buried her fingers in his hair and pulled back only long enough to tell him "If I stay, I won't be able to keep myself from doing this, either," before she kissed him back—harder this time. She sucked his lower lip in her mouth and bit down. He groaned and yanked up the hem of her sweater. And then her shirt. And then the T-shirt she had on underneath that. But eventually, he got to her bare skin and when he touched her there, she shivered.

"Are you cold?" he murmured against her skin.

She wasn't. She was burning with the heat that started at her core and radiated out. She had on far too much clothing—and so did he.

"Maybe."

He leaned back and, cupping her face in both his hands, stared at her. "If you're cold, maybe I should warm you."

Please let me be good enough for him. "Maybe you should."

Somehow, they made it up the stairs. It wasn't easy—she was trying to yank his sweater over his head and he was doing the same. And then there were the shirts underneath. Hands and mouths were everywhere as she jerked at buttons and he slid down the zipper on her pants. There was an advantage to wearing jeans that were too big for her—they skimmed over her long-underwear-clad hips and she was able to walk out of them in the middle of the hallway.

"Which way?" she asked because she'd only been in one room up here, the impersonal guest room.

She didn't want this to be impersonal. She wanted every single thing to be deeply personal—from the way that CJ was kissing her and skimming his teeth over her neck and biting down against her skin to the way the muscles of his stomach tensed when she scraped her nails over his shoulders.

"Here—wait." CJ leaned heavily against the door and pulled the last of her shirts off over her head. His eyes fell upon her bra. "Oh, Lord," he groaned as he stared at her breasts covered in lacy pink silk.

"They're not real," she said quickly before he touched them. She'd had them done for the beauty pageant circuit. Normally, she didn't tell people that—but he had asked for the truth. So, this was her being truthful. "I had implants years ago."

It took him several moments to drag his eyes up to hers. "You must've had a very good surgeon because I never would've guessed." He dropped his gaze again and lifted his hands. But he didn't touch her. Instead his fingertips hovered above her skin. "What can you feel?"

She pressed his hands against her bra. Automatically, he cupped her and dragged his thumbs over her nipples. "I can feel that," she breathed. After she'd gotten them done, there'd been a period where things hadn't felt the same. But that had been a long time ago and the sensations had come back.

He reached around her back and undid her bra. As it slid off, she shivered because this hallway was not warm. Her nipples went rock-hard and, in response, CJ made a noise deep in the back of his throat. A noise of hunger and need. "How about this?" He teased the tips of her nipples and Natalie couldn't help arching her back and thrusting her breasts closer to him.

"Oh, *yes*." CJ hadn't made a move to open the door and drag her onto the bed. Instead, he seemed content where he was, lavishing attention on her breasts.

"How about this?" he asked, his voice straining. Lightly, *lightly* he pinched one of her nipples between his thumb and forefinger, with just the slightest pressure. "Do you like that?"

She wouldn't have thought it possible to want him even more, but in that moment, she did. To him, she was a person with wants and needs and she knew that he would take care of her. She had always known it, ever since he'd picked her up and dragged her into his house and made sure she didn't freeze to death.

"Don't stop," she pleaded.

He didn't. He took his time stroking and tugging on her breasts. When he lowered his mouth and sucked one nipple between his lips, she couldn't stand it. She moaned and whimpered and held him against her. He let his teeth nip at her until she was nearly crazed with desire.

"CJ," she begged. "I can't take much more."

But still he didn't let her go. Instead, without pulling his mouth off of her, he slid his hand down between them. She still had on panties and a pair of long underwear, but that didn't stop him. His hand dipped below the waistbands of both and moved lower, until he was stroking her sex.

"I think you can," he murmured against her skin before his teeth scraped over the top of her breast and he latched onto her nipple again.

All she could do was hold on to his shoulders and watch as he suckled her. When he hit her very center with his fingers and began to make maddening circles, she bucked against him. He looked up at her, and in that moment, she was lost. She came undone in his arms as wave after wave of pleasure threatened to knock her legs out from under her.

But she didn't need to worry because as she sagged against him, CJ caught her in his arms. "You are so beautiful when you come," he whispered, and damn if his voice didn't have a reverential tone to it.

Her mouth opened because she felt like she should say something. Normally, she did. She came up with some semi-sincere compliment on her lover's skill or she exaggerated the orgasm that she might not have had.

But *this* orgasm had been actually mind-blowing and she couldn't form words. Instead of the heavy hollowness she was used to, she felt light and shimmery. Special and wonderful.

It was so unfamiliar but already, she knew she wanted more.

She wanted all of him.

He was so hard with desire that it was now physically painful—but it had been worth it. Real or not, her breasts were fabulous. And watching her come?

That had been honest. It had been one of the most exciting things in his entire life. He had rendered her speechless and that made him feel good.

Her hand brushed over his throbbing dick and that shattered the last of his self-control.

He swept her legs out from under her and got the door to his room open. Then they were falling into bed, a tangled mass of arms and legs. He stripped her down to her panties and then down to nothing at all. He wanted to take his time—but he didn't have any more time to take. This wasn't a thinking thing. They had blown past seduction and there was no turning back.

"Oh, CJ," she whispered when she finally freed him. He sprang to full attention and when her hands closed around him, he almost lost it. Because she was stroking him and he wasn't this strong.

"Babe, now," he said, forcing himself to pull away and reach for the bedside table. The condoms were probably still good even though it'd been a while. "How do you like it?"

A look of confusion temporarily blotted out the desire on her face. He had to wonder if anyone had ever asked her that. She needed better friends.

"I liked it when you played with my breasts," she said, her eyes wide as he rolled on the condom.

"Then you can be on top." And he'd have full access to her. He'd nearly made her come just by playing with her nipples—how much would she shatter if he did that while he was making love to her?

She straddled him. There was nothing slow or gentle about either of their movements. She guided him to her opening and he tweaked her nipples as he thrust into her and it was better than good. The way she surrounded him, all warm wetness? The way she tasted in his mouth? The little noises she made as he pulled her apart so he could drive up harder? He couldn't even call it great because it was so much better than that.

He surrendered himself to her completely. Her

pleasure was all his as she took him in and took him deeper. He filled his hands with her, stroking and sucking, licking and biting until she threw back her head and shuddered. He grabbed her by the hips and drove up into her, letting go as the climax tore through his body.

She collapsed down on him. They were breathing hard and a sheen of sweat covered them. "God, Natalie," he murmured as he lifted her off of him and slid her into the crook of his arm. He got rid of the condom and then pulled the covers up over them.

She was quiet and he wasn't sure if that was a good thing or not. He hoped he hadn't been too rusty for her.

"Stay with me," he said. "Stay with me for Christmas. Stay as long as you like."

She was quiet for a little while longer. "I can't. I wish I could but..."

It wasn't like her answer was a surprise or anything. Winters on the ranch were long—but they didn't last all year. And besides, eventually she'd get tired of his life. She'd want to go back to the comforts and conveniences of living in a big city instead of the isolation and hard work that went with ranching.

He accepted that. But what would happen when she left? It'd taken her less than four days to wind up in his bed. If she stayed through the New Year, how long would it take her to wind up in his heart?

Just like anything else with her, there was a risk.

But apparently, it was one he was going to take, common sense be damned.

"I doubt the snow is going to melt before New Year's Eve."

She propped herself up on her elbows and stared down at him, a strange mix of emotions playing out on her face. "And you'd be okay with that?"

What kind of question was that? Especially considering that they were lying nude in each other's arms?

He rolled into her, trapping her body underneath his. Even that simple movement made him hard again because he could feel the weight of her breasts underneath him and her legs sliding around his. He began to thrust slowly, dragging his erection over the outer folds of her sex.

"I want you," he told her as he grabbed her hands and pinned them by the side of her head. "I'm tired of fighting it. I want *you*."

"I'm not good enough for you," she whispered even as she began to writhe underneath him as he made contact with her over and over again. "I ruin everything."

"That's a lie," he told her. "Whoever told you that was lying." He let go of her long enough to fish another condom off the bedside table and roll it on. Then he positioned himself against her and, with one hard thrust, buried himself deep in her body. "You *are* good for me and I want you just the way you are."

And if he couldn't make her believe his words, by God, he was going to make her believe his actions. As he buried himself inside her, thrust after thrust, he showed her. He wanted her. Just her.

It was only later, when they were curled around each other under the covers and she was already asleep, that something occurred to him. She'd said she ruined everything—and it wasn't the first time she'd said it.

What if she hadn't been just repeating something that had been drummed into her when she'd been little?

What if she hadn't been talking about the past at all?

What if she had been telling him something about the future—*his* future?

Sleep was a long time coming.

Ten

Christmas Eve passed in a blur for Natalie. She helped feed the horses and rode the snowmobile with CJ out to different parts of his property. She got to watch him break ice on ponds for his cows. She had done a story not terribly long ago on the appeal of lumbersexuals. But watching CJ swing a sledgehammer? All of those muscles in action? *Damn*.

The day warmed up considerably. By the time they made it to the third pond, CJ had unzipped his snowsuit and had the upper part hanging around his waist while he broke ice. The snow was already beginning to melt, dripping off of trees and running in rivulets toward the ponds. Everything sparkled and was bright—but she knew what this thaw meant.

It was the beginning of the end. Once the snow melted, she wouldn't have a good reason to stay out here. Which was a shame, because they had just gotten started.

Once they made it back to the house, CJ spent a lot of time on the phone with his neighbors, making sure everything was ready for the parade and the party tonight. Then he disappeared upstairs and returned with a bright red sweatshirt and a pair of green sweatpants. He also had a more feminine-looking red top that had lace around the collar and bell sleeves. That was paired with a dark green skirt. He even had a pair of candy cane–striped tights. The last thing was a green-and-red-striped hat with a pair of elf ears attached. It was ridiculous—just looking at it made Natalie smile.

"All of this is going to be too big on you," he said, handing her the clothes. "If you put the sweats on over the snowsuit, you'll be good for the parade, and then at the party you can change into the other things. That is, if you don't mind playing my elf?" As he said that last part, the color in his face deepened. "You'll have to stand beside me and hand out presents to the kids."

She beamed at him. "I would love to be your elf," she said sincerely, trying the ears on. They felt silly—but good, too. Then something else occurred to her. "Does anyone else know I'm here?"

"I didn't tell anyone in town. I mean, I can, if

you'd like—they don't have to know you've been here for days, but we could say you're the special guest of honor."

A week ago, she would've demanded just that. The honorary grand marshal or something else that would've made her the center of attention.

That wasn't what she wanted now. She could play this Christmas party and her involvement in it for ratings and self-promotion—or she could let the focus be on Santa and the kids. She could be just an elf, handing out presents and waving in a parade.

"Don't tell anyone," she said. "I'm just one of Santa's helpers." Never in a million years had she thought she would ever say anything like that.

But then again, never in a million years would a man's smile have meant as much to her as CJ's did. "People might recognize you," he told her. "You did spend an awful lot of time at that diner."

She winced at the memory of wheedling and cajoling information out of the locals. "There's going to be talk, isn't there?"

But he just shrugged and pulled her into his arms and kissed her. "I don't think it'll be a problem," he said as she settled into his arms. "Firestone's been having this party for forty-two years—no one wants to mess with tradition."

She personally did not have a lot of faith in humanity. However, this was his town. All she could do at this point was hope for the best.

Still, after a quick dinner—CJ promised there would be food and drink at the party—Natalie suited up. She was back in the layers again *plus* the snowsuit *plus* the sweats. CJ helped her get the sweatshirt over her head—and now, because she had seen *A Christmas Story*, she understood what he meant when he asked, "Can you put your arms down now?"

"Funny," she told him as he loaded her change of clothes and her elf hat into a bag stuffed with pillows.

"I try," he said with a smirk. "Hold this." He gave her his Santa beard. The plan was for them to ride the snowmobile into town then ditch it before he put the beard on and rode an old-fashioned sleigh down the main street of Firestone.

The stack of pillows served two purposes. One, it would make it look like the sleigh was filled with a sack of toys in the parade. But the other purpose was more practical. With a Santa suit over his snowsuit, CJ didn't need the extra padding for the parade. However, there was no way he could sit in a snowsuit inside the community center for a couple of hours without dying of heat exhaustion. So he would use the pillows for his stomach once the party started.

It was a struggle for Natalie to hold on to the sack and the beard and CJ, and even though it had been warm today, it was still a long, cold ride into town. What would have taken twenty minutes in the car took close to an hour on the snowmobile. By the time they eased into Firestone, her nose was running and her cheeks were frozen.

"This way," CJ said, parking on a snow-covered side street and helping her off the snowmobile.

"Aren't you going to take the keys?" she asked as he led her away.

He shook his head. "Everyone knows that's my vehicle. This isn't Denver, you know. Jamie!" he called out as they turned the corner. "We're here!"

Natalie stumbled to a stop. A short parade—no more than fifteen floats—stretched out along the narrow street of downtown Firestone. They came upon the rear, where an actual sleigh—with actual reindeer—waited for them. Some of the floats were on flatbed trailers that were being hauled by tractors so large they took up the entire street. There were more horse-drawn sleighs and even a couple of people dressed up like clowns on cross-country skis.

All Natalie could do was stand and stare, her mouth open. The whole thing was unreal—but in the best way possible. CJ hadn't been exaggerating. This dinky little town in the middle of nowhere put on a Christmas extravaganza every single year and it was...

It was simply the most magical thing she'd ever seen.

"Ready?" CJ had gotten his beard on while she'd patted the neck of a reindeer and suddenly, he was Santa. He *definitely* had the twinkle in his eye.

"My ears." He helped get her hood and ski mask off and then crammed the stocking cap with the attached elf ears onto her head. Then he and someone Natalie only vaguely recognized from the diner helped her up into the sleigh. The reindeer shifted nervously until CJ took the reins.

"Miss, do you think you can stand and wave?" Jamie asked as he handed the sack of pillows up to CJ.

Natalie braced her feet and her knees and gripped the back of CJ's seat. "We're about to find out," she said with a huge grin.

Jamie stepped back. "Meet you all at the community center," he called out.

The parade in front of them moved and CJ flicked the reins. Slowly, they made their public appearance as Santa Claus and his elf.

It took a block before they reached any parade watchers, but when they did, Natalie guessed that the entire town of Firestone had made it for this event. Kids bundled up in thick coats and hats and boots stood on the sidewalks, waving and shouting as CJ came into view. Clearly, the reindeer had done this before because the noise didn't seem to faze them at all. And Natalie? She managed to keep her balance and wave and smile at all of the kids.

Magical didn't begin to describe this feeling of happiness that started midchest and radiated outward. Nobody recognized her. But strangely, they

lidn't have to. All of her fame and notoriety mattered
for exactly nothing right now. It should have been
terrifying—but it wasn't. All that mattered was the
way the kids clapped and cheered as CJ *ho-ho-ho-*
ed his way through downtown Firestone.

Then, as quickly as it had begun, the parade was
over and CJ was helping her out of the sleigh. They
had parked behind a building that she assumed was
the community center and a woman who looked exactly like Mrs. Claus opened the door for them. "Oh,
thank goodness," she said. "Hurry! They're going to
be here for hot cocoa any second."

"Doreen," CJ said, "could you show her where the
ladies room is? I've got to get out of this snowsuit."
With that, he hurried down the hallway.

"This way, dearie," Doreen said as she led Natalie
in the opposite direction. "Thank you so much for
being an elf. The children do so enjoy this."

"I'm having an amazing time," Natalie said honestly. Because she was. She hadn't believed that
things like this were still possible in today's world.
Childlike innocence and joy... Who knew?

As she struggled out of her layers, Natalie could
hear the noise begin to rise in the building. Undoubtedly, families were flooding into the warmth and demanding hot chocolate and cookies. As she took off
her elf ears and rearranged her hair so that it would
be entirely hidden under the hat, a band started playing Christmas songs.

She braced herself and looked in the mirror. The candy-cane tights sealed the deal, she decided. That and the ears. Days ago, the thought of anyone seeing her dressed like this would've been horrifying. But right now it seemed like the perfect outfit. She *was* an elf.

She found Doreen in the kitchen again. "They're going to announce him in a minute," Doreen whispered. "When he comes down the hall, you can join him. The presents are arranged by size. The big flat presents are for the toddlers, the thin ones are for the middle schoolers and the heavy books are for the teenagers." Natalie must have given her a look because the older woman patted her on the arm and said, "CJ will know who gets what."

I hope so, Natalie thought as she peeked at the party. Senior citizens sat at tables and sipped punch and eggnog while kids and teenagers bopped around the postage stamp–sized dance floor. Desserts filled tables all along one wall—and people were eating them almost as fast as Doreen could carry them out.

When the song ended, the band started playing another song to introduce Santa Claus. All the kids began to cheer as the lead singer announced, "Here he is, boys and girls, all the way from the North Pole, it's the man of the hour—Santa Claus and his elf, Jingles!"

Jingles? Natalie grinned as the band dropped its volume down to a whisper and the entire room seemed to hold its breath. Natalie was no exception. She was watching the hallway, waiting for her cue.

One moment the hallway was empty. The next, here he was, *ho-ho-ho-ing* as he strode into the room. Natalie fell into step behind him as the entire room erupted into cheers. Adults and kids clapped as they headed over to a corner of the room that had been decorated with an enormous chair surrounded by piles of presents.

It was just *crazy*. She took her place next to this *throne*—the only word she could use to describe it. Some of the parents with the smallest children jockeyed to be first on Santa's lap. But CJ smiled and laughed and took time with each kid and then pointed to the book he wanted Natalie to hand over.

Through it all she smiled and giggled and nodded as Jingles. With every gift she handed over and every picture she took—because a lot of parents were handing her their cell phones so they could crowd in the picture behind CJ—she laughed. She was laughing more tonight than she had in years. And laughing was easy. It was *fun*. There was no tightness in her chest, no clawing worry about what people were thinking, what they were saying about her. Because she knew. They were coming up to her and thanking her for being a part of the night, thanking her for making the kids smile—especially the ones who were a little scared of the big man in the white beard.

Nobody knew who she was. And it was the most

freeing thing she'd ever experienced. But more than that, people were nice to her for no reason. They weren't going to get anything out of it, other than a fun family evening. And the same went for her.

She hadn't thought that people could still be nice. But the entire town of Firestone was proving her wrong.

After two hours of intense Santa-ing, the community center began to empty out. Families had to get their children to bed so Santa could get to work filling stockings, and the older people had a long way to travel. CJ and Natalie weren't the only ones who'd come in on snowmobiles and it was going to be a dark trip back.

When the crowd was gone, CJ looked up at her and patted his lap. Natalie sat, grateful for the break. Happiness took a lot of effort.

"And what do you want for Christmas, little girl?" he asked, grinning widely behind his fake beard.

Natalie pretended to think about it. More than anything, she didn't want this time with him to end. "I don't suppose I could ask for another blizzard?"

Something in his eyes changed—deepened—and Natalie felt warm all over. "Here," he said, reaching underneath his seat and pulling out her—

Her phone.

She looked up at him in surprise. "You've been a very good girl," he said and then he winked at her.

She stared down at her phone. "Are you sure?" Because she'd half assumed he'd destroyed it—anything to keep her from exposing him.

And now he was giving it back to her. In one piece, even.

He didn't kiss her. It probably wouldn't do for Santa Claus to be seen cheating on Mrs. Claus with an elf. But he gave her a little squeeze. "I trust you," he said in his real voice, low and for her ears only.

Then another family approached and Natalie hopped up to get back to work. She almost didn't turn the phone on. She wouldn't have even thought about it if he hadn't given it to her.

A couple of men Natalie recognized from her time at the diner came up to CJ. "I need something to drink," she told him and he nodded and smiled as he turned his attention to his friends. She could only hope they weren't warning him about her.

As she sipped a foam cup full of cooling cocoa, she stared at her phone. The temptation to turn it on was huge. Huge. But what if she did? What would be waiting for her? All the trolling vitriol that she'd come to expect? Angry emails from her producer, Steve, demanding to know where she and her story were? For a second, she even considered that her dad might've tried to call her and wish her happy Christmas.

But worse—what if it was silence? No notifications, no messages? No…nothing?

She didn't want to see what people had been saying and she didn't want them not to have said anything at all. God, what a mess. And this was her life.

Behind her, CJ laughed with his friends. None of these people knew he was a Beaumont. It didn't matter that he wasn't famous. He was liked. That was…

That was more valuable than she'd realized it was.

A sense of peace filled her. Maybe she didn't need likes and shares. Maybe she just needed him. She looked at the silly decorations and the sugar cookies and all the smiling people who'd slogged through snow to celebrate this time with each other. With her.

She never wanted it to end.

But of course, it had to. Nothing lasted forever, not even snow in December. She'd have to go back and tell her producer…something. She still didn't know what. But when she left…

She wanted a memory. Just one to remind her of the Christmas she'd spent with a grumpy, sexy cowboy. It would be enough. More than she'd had before she'd come to this town.

As casually as she could, she turned on her phone and closed her eyes against the notifications. She opened the camera app and snapped a picture of CJ sitting on his throne. She caught him at just the right moment—his friends had moved out of the frame, but he wasn't looking at her.

She stared down at the picture. All she saw was Santa. The only parts of CJ that were visible were his eyes and she didn't think even his own mother would be able to pick him out of a Santa lineup.

But she'd know. She'd always know.

Quickly, she turned the phone back off before she lost her willpower and started tapping through to the social media apps.

When she glanced back at CJ, she caught him watching her. Guilt whispered that she should tell him she took the photo but she decided against it. It was for her and her alone. A perfect memory of a perfect Christmas.

Someone came up to her and asked for an official photo of her and CJ for the county newspaper, so she put on her big smile and went to stand by him. Everything was fine.

But through it all, she couldn't shake one nagging feeling.

She ruined everything. She always had.

Would she ruin this, too?

Eleven

CJ woke up early—he always did on Christmas. Natalie was still fast asleep. It was Christmas morning and she wasn't under the tree, but he'd gotten what he'd asked for.

He grinned at himself. There was something not quite right about Santa asking himself for a present. But he wanted Natalie. And when she had asked for more snow instead of her phone?

This probably wasn't love. The thing was, though, he wasn't one hundred percent sure that it *wasn't* love. The only other time he'd thought he'd been in love, he'd been wrong.

He watched her sleep. The ride home from the

party last night had been long and cold and he didn't want to wake her.

His thoughts turned to another Christmas, one about twenty years ago. He'd been thirteen and Hardwick Beaumont had made headlines *again* for divorcing another wife and keeping the children. CJ had always been dimly aware that Dad wasn't actually his birth father because his mother had drilled it into his head that he was never to go anywhere with anyone named Beaumont. And he was dimly aware of the story his parents told everyone about how they met—his dad had been visiting Denver on leave from his stint in the army, met his mom and fallen in love so fast that he had married her quickly before he finished his tour of duty. After his honorable discharge, Pat had returned to Denver to find his wife waiting with an infant CJ. The way the story went, it was one of those love-at-first-sight things.

But that wasn't the truth. They hadn't met while Pat was on leave—they had met after Pat's discharge. CJ had already been four months old and his mom was desperate. Her family was deeply religious and when she'd gotten pregnant with him they'd disowned her. Apparently, Hardwick Beaumont had given her some hush money, but it was starting to run out and she hadn't known what she was going to do until the handsome young soldier walked into her life.

CJ's parents had only told him the true story once,

but he had never forgotten it. Even at the age of thirteen, he'd paid close attention.

It had not been love at first sight. Isabel Santino had seen a handsome young man who bore a passing resemblance to her child's father. But more than that, she had seen a handsome young man who would protect her and CJ. And Pat? His parents had died while he was in the service. He was suddenly in charge of a massive ranching operation that had been neglected for eight months. He had needed a ranch wife, basically. Isabel had applied for a job but somehow, she'd convinced Pat to marry her and give her son his name.

Pat had not formally adopted CJ until he was three. By that time, Pat and Bell Wesley had fallen in love. The adoption, more than the wedding, had been the promise to love and protect their family, until death did they part. Not that anyone had known about the adoption, of course.

At least, they hadn't until recently. There'd only been a few whispers that'd reached his ears last night during the party—a few warnings that someone was looking for him and spreading rumors that he was a Beaumont, not Pat's son. But people had been too preoccupied with the band and the spiked eggnog and CJ had managed to deflect any further questions with a simple "Yeah, I heard. I'm not worried." And he hadn't been.

As he stared down at Natalie, her face soft with

sleep, he wondered what the hell was going on between them. He honestly could not figure out if he was glad that she had barged into his life or not. If she hadn't barged in, no one would ever have connected him with the Beaumont family.

But then she wouldn't be here with him now. He wouldn't be wondering if there could be something more between them. Something that looked like love.

He slipped out of bed. Out of the barn, he had the almost-finished wooden star he'd carved for his mom. He'd made up his mind—he was going to give it to Natalie instead. He meant to put one more coat of lacquer on it, but he could give it a light sanding now and put it under the tree. She hadn't told him the details of her childhood—not in so many words. But watching her last night—hell, over the last several days—had made one thing clear.

She hadn't known what Christmas truly was. And he had to wonder if anyone had ever given her a gift. A real gift, one that had meaning and hope.

She meant something to him. He didn't have the precise label for it. But he didn't need one.

As he suited up and headed out to the barn to feed his horses and sand the star, he could only hope that he meant something to her, too.

Natalie woke up alone. Even though that was how she normally woke up in her own place, it still felt unusual here. It shouldn't be possible that she missed CJ already, but she did.

For a few moments, she lay there reliving not the Christmas morning her mom had left and not every painful Christmas call with her father in the last decade. For the first time in…well, forever—she had happy memories.

Everything about last night had been magical. The sleigh ride down the middle of Firestone, handing out presents as Jingles—coming home with CJ and falling into bed with him…

It was perfect. Too perfect, almost. There was such a sense of joy and peace surrounding her and CJ and this time that it felt dangerous.

Last night, he'd made her feel special and wonderful. He'd lavished affection upon her—God, she'd never known sex could be *that* good.

She'd never been in love. Honestly, it scared her a little bit. She wasn't good enough for him. But, CJ being CJ, he made her think that maybe…

What was she doing? It was Christmas morning! Full of hope and happiness and excitement! She might only ever get one shot at a perfect Christmas morning with a perfect cowboy and she wasn't about to waste it lounging alone in bed. Besides, CJ was right—there was no future and no past. There was just today.

And today—like yesterday and last night—was

going to be a gift. One she would treasure for the rest of her days.

Downstairs, she found CJ in the kitchen, sipping coffee. His cheeks were red and he had a strange smile on his face, one she couldn't interpret.

"Hi," she said.

"Merry Christmas," he said as he pulled her into his arms and kissed her fiercely.

She sank into his kiss. In the here and now, at least, she had this and by God, she wouldn't ruin it.

"I think Santa brought you something," CJ said when the kiss finally ended.

Natalie shot him a questioning look, but he didn't elaborate. Instead, he put his hand on her lower back and guided her toward the living room. He'd already plugged in the lights and he'd gotten a fire going. Natalie prayed for more than just a little snow.

She wasn't sure she ever wanted to leave. Not this place and not CJ.

"How long have you been up?" she asked, marveling at the scene before her.

For there, underneath the tree, was something small and golden. It hadn't been there yesterday.

"Go on," CJ said.

"But I didn't get you anything," she protested as she kneeled and picked up the...

It was a star, a perfect golden star—the Christmas star. As she held it in her hands, her heart swelled.

He had given her so much…but this? A gift under the tree for *her*?

Her eyes filled with tears. "It's beautiful," she told him, blinking as fast as she could. From this moment on, she would always have a tree and she would always hang the star on it, no matter what. "I don't deserve this."

"*You* are beautiful, and I think you do," he replied, crouching beside her and putting his arm around her shoulders. "Natalie, I know this hasn't been exactly normal, us getting to know each other, and I know you have to go back to your life in Denver, but…"

She stared at him. He was serious. Not only was he giving her the perfect Christmas, but he also wanted to see more of her.

Oh, God. She'd never fallen in love, never dreamed she could find someone who might possibly care for her in return—even a little bit.

But she was falling for him. He was good and kind and thoughtful and…

And she wasn't. She was still Natalie Baker, wasn't she? What if he put all this faith in her and believed that she was a good person and…

And she ruined it, just like she ruined everything?

"If you want to keep seeing each other…" he said, looking downright shy.

She should say no. She should end this while it was still perfect, before she did something that made him hate her. Because she would. That was who she was and she had promised not to lie to him. Not anymore.

But *no* was not what came out of her mouth. Maybe she was weak. Maybe it was the fact that this was the best Christmas she could remember. Maybe she was just selfish.

Whatever it was, she said, "*Yes*. I want to keep doing this." All of it—not just Christmas. Riding out with him on his snowmobile. Feeding the horses. Snuggling under a blanket and watching movies. Even going to town and celebrating with all of his friends and neighbors—and especially coming home and going to bed with him. She wanted it all.

She'd always wanted things she knew she couldn't have—a happy family, friends who cared, a man she could love. He made everything feel like it was *possible*.

She kissed him—hard. So hard, in fact, that she knocked him over. She pulled at his clothes and he stripped hers off in a frenzy. He wanted her. She didn't deserve him but she wanted him, too.

She wouldn't screw it up. He was the best gift she ever could have asked for.

They made love in front of the fire while the Christmas lights twinkled in the background. Afterward, they lay in each other's arms and, for the first time, talked about the future. He could come down and spend the night at her place and she could come up on the weekends when she was done tap-ing her show.

Her show...

No. She pushed that note of panic away even as she knew she couldn't avoid harsh reality forever.

She tightened her arms around CJ's waist and forced her thoughts to focus on the good things. CJ wanted to keep seeing her. They'd be together.

Oh, yes—she wanted to keep doing *this*.

That glow only lasted for so long. By the time they finished watching *Miracle on 34th Street*, doubt had slithered back into her mind in full force.

It was Christmas day. The one day a year when she called her father.

For a moment, she almost decided she wouldn't do it. Why did she have to?

But it was Christmas and he was her father. At least he'd stuck around. So she sort of owed him.

"I'm going to call my dad to wish him merry Christmas," Natalie said but she couldn't even man-age to sound excited about it.

CJ noticed. "Are you sure?"

Of course she wasn't sure. They had been having a wonderful Christmas and she didn't want something like reality barging in on it. Who knew how much more time they had in this protective little bubble?

"No," she admitted, shooting him a weak smile. "But I don't want to give up on him. He's all I've got." She leaned over to get her phone, which had spent most of the day on the middle of the coffee table, silent and black.

CJ pulled her back. "That's not true," he told her, cupping her cheek and looking her in the eye. "You have me."

God, how she wanted that to be true. "CJ..." she whispered, brushing her lips over his.

"Go," he told her. "Call your dad." Then he got up and headed toward the kitchen to give her some privacy.

She didn't call, not right away. She opened up the camera app and cropped the photo she'd taken of CJ in his Santa suit. She saved it as her home screen with a smile.

But then she couldn't put it off any longer. She'd said she'd call and so she would.

The phone rang. And rang. Just as she was moving the phone away from her ear to end the call, her dad's scratchy voice crackled over the line. "What do you want?"

"Daddy?"

"Who is this?"

"It's me," she said, dread rising up in her stomach. "Natalie." Silence. "Your daughter?"

"Yeah, so?"

She swallowed down against the rising tide of panic. Why did she do this? Why did she try, year after year?

But then she stared at the Christmas tree with the bright lights, at her golden star glowing right in the middle. This wasn't the normal way she spent Christmas, alone in her sterile condo. She wasn't her normal self, either. She was better now.

"I wanted to call and wish you a merry Christmas, Daddy."

There was a painful silence. "You just gotta rub it in my face, don't you? Every year, you gotta call and remind me that this is the day she left. And you know why?"

"Why?" she asked in a shaking voice, unable to blink fast enough. She tried to put his words into context. He was slurring. He'd probably been drinking. He was upset. He was…

He wasn't done yet.

"Because you ruined Christmas, girl. And every year, you gotta call me up and remind me that I wasn't enough for her because she couldn't deal with a spoiled brat like you."

And with that, he hung up.

Natalie sat there, pain blossoming in her chest until she was nothing but regret.

Of course she ruined everything. Always had, always would. See? She'd even ruined her own Christmas because she thought she was doing a nice thing by reaching out to her father.

She'd thought…

What a fool she'd been, she suddenly realized.

She'd thought she could be someone else and why? Because CJ treated her like a decent human? Ha. She'd never change. Even her father said so.

She was a former runner-up beauty queen with fake boobs and more wrinkles than she could keep at bay. She had nothing but her show. No family. No friends.

She had CJ...

But did she, really? This had been a great week. A nice vacation. But when she went back to her soulless condo and her fake morning smiles and her battles with Kevin and Steve over ratings, would she really have CJ?

No. Their lives were too far apart. If she gave up everything for him, she'd be left with nothing.

She needed her show. It was all she had.

She opened the photo app and looked at CJ in his Santa suit. Insecurity clobbered her on the back of the head and almost knocked her flat. She couldn't breathe.

Everything was wrong.

But she knew one thing she could do to make things right.

Even as it occurred to her, her stomach turned, but she didn't stop to think about how he was different, how he cared for her, how he trusted her...

He was the one thing that would keep her show going. The *only* thing.

She cropped the photo and uploaded it to Instagram. Guess who's behind the beard? she typed, then tagged her producer and hit Share.

But instead of the normal pop of excitement that normally went with posting, she felt sick to her stomach. So she turned off her phone. She didn't want to see the notifications.

Besides, it was Christmas. A Santa teaser was the perfect thing to post. It wasn't a big deal. No one would know it was him, anyway.

And she had to keep her show. It was all she had.

Natalie had been quiet ever since she'd called her dad. CJ had asked if everything was all right, but she'd just curled into his side and asked him to start another movie. So he'd loaded up *The Santa Clause* and they watched it in near silence.

It hurt him that her father had obviously wished Natalie anything but a merry Christmas. But she didn't want to talk about it, so he didn't push.

The movie was nearing the end when his phone buzzed. "It's probably my folks," he said, kissing her as he climbed off the couch.

"You want to pause the movie?" She gave him a smile that was almost convincing.

"No, you keep watching, babe. I'll be right back."

Except it wasn't his parents on the phone. "CJ?" It was his half brother, Zeb Richards.

"Is everything all right?" CJ asked automatically,

trying to figure out why Zeb was calling him. Maybe
he wanted to wish him a merry Christmas?

But even as he thought it, CJ knew that wasn't it.
They did not have what a reasonable person might
consider a "close brotherly relationship." In fact, the
only time they had communicated outside of the
meeting Zeb had called months ago about his pro-
posed takeover of the Beaumont Brewery had been
the message CJ had sent a few days ago.

"Depends on your definition of 'all right,'" Zeb
said. "It appears Natalie Baker has decided you are
a story after all."

She had? This was news to him. "Are you sure?
She's been with me for the last week. She got snowed
in and I haven't been able to get her out."

True, he had stopped trying to get her out several
days ago. But still—she'd been here.

"I'm sending you a link," Zeb said, tactfully ignoring the implications of CJ and Natalie being
snowed in together. "Daniel is already writing a press
release acknowledging that you are one of our brothers, but you value your privacy, et cetera, et cetera,
et cetera. He didn't want to release it without your
approval. I've also spoken with Chadwick. He told
me that whatever you'd like to happen, you'll have
his help. So if you want to be publicly announced as
a Beaumont, we can make that happen. And if not,
we'll do our best to bury the lede."

A link? And Zeb had been talking with Chadwick? Daniel had already worked up a press release? "You know it's Christmas, right?"

"Trust me, I know. I'm hiding in my study from my wife. She informed me that I was not allowed to work today—but," he continued, sighing heavily, "this is important. You're family." Before CJ could even process *that*, Zeb said, "I'm also supposed to tell you that next year, you're invited to Christmas dinner. Casey's a little miffed that we didn't have the entire family over, although I told her I wanted our first Christmas to be just us."

CJ couldn't think a year ahead. Right now, he couldn't even think a minute ahead. "Are you sure?"

About any of it? How would Natalie have even gotten the story out? He'd been sitting on her phone for days and they hadn't been apart since he'd given it back to her. The whole day, it'd been on the coffee table.

And it wasn't easy for him to think of the Beaumonts—even ones who didn't have the same last name—as family. He understood that they were blood relatives, but he wasn't sure he wanted to give up being a Wesley.

"You can let me know," Zeb said in the silence. "But we're going to have to have an official response in a day or so. Sooner would be better. Daniel believes we need to get out in front of this before it gets out of hand."

"Yeah," CJ said, feeling numb as he ended the

all. It wasn't just that he didn't know how Natalie might've gotten the word out to anyone about him. It was that...

Well, he thought he'd changed her mind. It hadn't been an explicit goal, certainly not during the first few days they'd been stuck in the living room together. But she hadn't pried. She hadn't asked questions. She hadn't demanded answers. Instead, she'd been vulnerable and fragile but also tough and unflappable. She'd rolled with the changes and embraced his chores and his town's party. She'd embraced *him*.

Hadn't she?

Or had it all been an act?

Seconds later, his phone pinged with a link. Dread churning his stomach, he clicked on it.

"Who's behind the beard?" It was a talking head that CJ vaguely recognized as Kevin Durante, another morning regular on Natalie's station. "Next on a special edition of *A Good Morning with Natalie Baker*." The show's theme music played as the graphics flashed across the screen. CJ felt sicker with each passing second.

Then the camera focused on the handsome man. "Good morning, Denver. I'm Kevin Durante, in for Natalie Baker, who is on assignment. Our top story— has the missing Beaumont bastard been found?"

CJ's stomach clenched at that—*on assignment*. *He* was her assignment. And there it was—a pic-

ture of CJ sitting on Santa's throne. He recognize
himself instantly.

CJ just stared at his phone. When had she take
the photo? He tried to run through the evening. It'
been such a flood of kids and parents and peopl
spiking their eggnog… Wait. There'd been a break
He'd given her the phone and then she'd gone to ge
something to drink. And he'd talked with Dale an
Larry for a little bit. That had to have been it.

She'd taken that photo and uploaded it. Kevi
showed the original Instagram post. Because h
didn't have anything else to say, he also read throug
some of the comments. There were the same sort o
comments CJ had seen the one time he'd looked a
the notifications on her phone. The whole thing dis
gusted him.

Kevin kept talking. There were "reports" that the
man behind the beard was CJ Wesley of Firestone
Colorado. But no one could confirm or deny tha
fact. Due to the weather, he explained, no one had
been able to get to Firestone and none of the Beaumonts were talking.

"We'll have more on this developing story soon,"
Kevin announced cheerfully.

It was all CJ could do to watch the clip again.
This was it. The moment his world changed forever.

That feeling only got stronger when Natalie
walked into the kitchen. She still looked upset. Well,
she could just be upset. He didn't even know if she

ad actually called her dad or if she had just checked
n with the station.

"Well?" He was real proud of the way he man-
ged to say that without his voice shaking with anger.

She didn't answer. Instead, she came straight to
is arms and buried her face against his chest. "The
novie was fine," she said, her voice muffled. "But I
wish I hadn't called my dad. I…I'm letting him ruin
my day and I shouldn't. I shouldn't."

It galled him how upset she sounded. Worse, it
galled him when his arms came around her without
is permission and held her tight.

Had any of it been real? He had only asked her for
two things. He had asked her not to pry into his life
and he had asked her for the truth. And she hadn't
been able to give him either.

Still, he clung to this moment because he knew
that as soon as he pushed her away, it was all over.
The bubble around them had burst and Christmas
would be over in a few short hours and everything
would go back to the way it had been before she'd
arrived.

He would go back to being alone. To hiding himself so that no one would know his secret. Well, it
was all over. The horse was out of that barn and there
was no shutting the door behind it.

She leaned back and looked up at him, her eyes
watery. "How about you? How are your parents?"

For a little while, his fantasy girl had fit into

his fantasy world. And now that while was over. "
wouldn't know."

She looked at him in confusion. "Then who
called?"

"My brother." The word still felt awkward in his
mouth, but he was going to have to get used to it now.

"Did he call to wish you a happy Christmas?"

CJ shook his head. Then he held up his phone and
hit the play button.

It took all of three seconds for her to realize what
she was watching—three of the longest seconds of
his life. Then her gaze met his, her eyes so wide—
and filled with something that looked a lot like fear.

"Turn it off."

"Why? This is why you came, isn't it?"

All the blood drained out of her face and she
began to tremble. "No," she said. It came out as a
plaintive wail. "It's not what I wanted."

He just shook his head. "You're on assignment.
Your boy Kevin said so himself."

"No," she said with more force. "I didn't think…
I assumed— They weren't supposed to do anything
with the photo until I got back. It was just a teaser.
And I was trying to figure out how I could… I don't
know." She seemed at a loss. "How I could redirect
the attention."

"Redirect it? Come on, Natalie," he scoffed.
"You're *all* about the attention, aren't you? You actually like it when people say those horrible things

you, don't you?" He saw her throat work as she wallowed, but she didn't say anything. "Well," he aid decisively, "you got what you came for. I'll see bout getting you back to Denver tomorrow."

Tears leaked out the corners of her eyes, but he vasn't going to be moved by them. For all he knew, he could cry on demand.

He should walk away. He was done with her and e wasn't about to give her a single thing more that he or anyone else could use.

But, dammit, it hurt to stand there and watch her ry to put on a brave face. She swallowed again. "That would be for the best. I'm sorry that I've intruded on your holiday."

Liar, he wanted to say. Because he knew her tell. He'd thought—for a little while—that he'd known *her*. "All I asked of you was to be honest."

"I was," she said with more force. "I *was*—except hat I made a mistake. I called my dad and he was terrible and I—I panicked. I don't have anything but my show. Without it, I'm nothing."

CJ let out a bark of laughter. "A mistake is an accident, Natalie. You can't convince me that you *accidentally* took a photo and then *accidentally* uploaded it across social media and that your coworkers *accidentally* did a four-minute segment on me."

She squeezed her eyes shut. "It was a mistake," she whispered. "Finding you, coming here—I

warned you. I'm nothing but a selfish, spoiled bra
and I ruin *everything*."

The last time she'd said that, he'd disagreed wit
her. This time, though, he didn't. She hadn't swal
lowed. She wasn't lying.

She dropped her head into her hands and dug th
heels of her palms into her eyes. "I wish you'd take
a hatchet to my phone. God, I wish you had destroye
the thing."

"So do I," he said bitterly. "So do I."

Twelve

The next twenty-four hours were some of the most miserable of Natalie's life. She slept in the guest room—alone, of course. CJ stopped talking to her completely. Not that she could blame him—she couldn't. But it was unnerving, the way he watched her. His eyes were cold and his expression was one step removed from a full-scale scowl—and it was directed at her at all times. She felt like a mouse with a hawk watching her.

She knew she had done this to herself. But she was also pissed off at her producer and at Kevin. They had taken *her* photo and made it *his* story. She had thought that Steve would have the decency to at least wait until she could make it back to the studio—but he hadn't. He hadn't even checked in with her before he had taken her story and run with it. She had been cut out almost completely.

The writing was on the wall. She was going to lose her show.

The whole reason she'd gone looking for CJ in the first place had been to save her show. She'd found him and yet she was going to lose her show anyway.

She had nothing.

One of the few things CJ said to her was that she had to dig out her car while he used his backhoe to plow the remaining snow off the drive. She didn't want to be in the house alone and obviously, CJ didn't want her in there, either. She had dressed in her own clothes that morning for the first time in days, but she put on the snowsuit and headed out. It was another warm day and everything was wet and slushy—which meant the snow was back-breakingly heavy. But she didn't mind. It took all of her concentration to excavate her tires and, when she'd done that, she started trying to dig tracks to a plowed section.

She had to leave. She knew that. But even as she hefted shovel after shovel of snow, she wished she didn't have to go. If only she'd held on to sanity through that moment of panic and insecurity. If only she'd had faith in CJ. If only…

If only she'd been someone else. Someone good enough for him.

But she wasn't, so she kept digging. Once she had

unearthed her car and CJ had unearthed the road, he hitched her car to his tractor and pulled it out. It was the last time she was alone with him, riding in the cab of his backhoe as he towed her car to the county road. The tension was a living thing because she had to sit on his knee, basically, but he didn't want to touch her.

Once they were at the road, she stripped out of the snowsuit and handed it back to him. Then she held out the star he'd made her. "Here—you keep this."

He looked offended. "I'm not taking it back. I gave it to you in good faith." Every word he said was another splinter in her skin because her faith had not been good. Not even close. "It's yours. Just don't put it on TV." He turned to go.

She couldn't let it end. Not like this. "CJ?"

He didn't look back. But he did stop. "What?"

She took a deep breath. "This was the best Christmas I've ever had."

"Sure it was." He started to walk.

She should just get in her car and drive off—but she couldn't. "CJ?" she called out after him.

"What, Natalie?" He turned, his hands on his hips, and glared at her.

"I'm sorry."

Something in his face changed, but at this distance, she couldn't make out what it was. Without another word, he turned and climbed into the backhoe.

She stood there and watched until he'd rumbled around a curve in the drive.

He didn't look back.

"Are you sure you're all right?" his mom asked for the thirtieth time. "We can come home. We can get through this together, sweetie."

CJ stifled a groan. He'd finally bitten the bullet and video-called to tell his parents that the cat was out of the bag. He loved his parents—he did—but he just wanted to brood in peace and quiet while he still could. Being fussed over by his mother wouldn't make anything better.

"I'm fine," he repeated. "Daniel Lee—remember him? One of my half brothers? He wrote the press release and he's handling it. I talked it over with him and we agreed it would be better if you guys stayed in Arizona until this blew over. If you come home now, it will only add fuel to the fire and everyone's going to want an interview."

He could see his mother physically recoil at the idea of doing interviews about Hardwick Beaumont and what had happened thirty-four years ago. She had lived as Bell Wesley for so long that everything that had come before Pat had happened to someone else, it seemed to CJ. And he couldn't blame her. Who the hell wanted to have to explain what they were doing when they'd had an affair decades ago? Hell, he shuddered at the thought of his college girlfriend—up

ntil now, the only other person who knew about his
onnection with the Beaumonts—coming out of the
oodwork and dishing on their relationship.

But he knew that his mother was hurting for him.
nd he hadn't even told his folks about how deep
e'd gotten with Natalie—or how much he was pay-
ig for that mistake.

"Well…" she said hesitantly.

"Son," Dad said, crowding into the camera's win-
ow. "We'll do what you want. We trust your judg-
ient on this and if you say that you and your half
rothers have the situation under control, then we're
oing to take you at your word." His mother looked
oubtful, but she didn't disagree. "In fact," Dad went
n diplomatically, "we were talking about pulling
ip stakes with the motorhome and driving over to
New Mexico for a little while. Your mother would
ike to see Santa Fe."

"That would be great," CJ said, hoping he hadn't
orced the enthusiasm past the point of believability.
His parents mostly wintered in Arizona, but every
now and then they did make side trips. Everyone
n Firestone had a general idea of where they were
n Arizona—but if they were in New Mexico, they
would be even more insulated from any fallout. "You
guys go and have fun, okay?"

They said their goodbyes and CJ ended the call.
Then he sat there in the silence of his big, empty
house and *brooded*. He put the odds of his parents

showing up at fifty percent. Sooner or later, h
mother would demand that they come home an
check on him.

He'd deal with that when he had to—there wer
more pressing concerns. Now that the road was clea
into town, he needed to make a supply run. But h
didn't want to. Because there would be question
and maybe even reporters. For a half second, C
wondered if Natalie would still be in Firestone, dig
ging up dirt and wielding her charms like a weapo

He had been *such* an idiot. That was the only log
ical conclusion. He had known what she was. Sh
had been right—she *had* warned him. But he had le
himself get swept up in the holidays and in her bi
eyes and her soft body. He had let himself be con
vinced that Natalie the woman was distinctly sepa
rate from Natalie Baker, morning television host. H
had always trusted his gut in these sorts of things—
but this was the second time that his gut had let hin
down when it came to women.

All he'd ever wanted was to be a Wesley and th
world simply wouldn't let him. It didn't matter tha
his dad was a good man or that CJ had done his bes
to follow his father's example. All that would eve
matter was that once upon a time his mother ha
conceived him with Hardwick Beaumont.

He had even had a phone call from the patriarc
of the Beaumont family, such as it was—Chadwic
Beaumont himself, welcoming CJ to the family an

assuring him that, no matter what level of involvement he wanted, he had the full support of the Beaumonts. CJ had honestly told his oldest half brother that he still wasn't sure what he wanted from any of them.

What had happened next still had CJ's head spinning. Chadwick had apologized for not contacting CJ when he'd located him three years ago.

Chadwick had known where he was—*who* he was—for three years. The news had rocked CJ. He had lived his entire life under the impression that he was unfindable. Yes, his mother had prepared him for the day one of the Beaumonts might locate him and do apparently nefarious things—but he'd never actually believed that would happen.

But he'd been wrong. Because Chadwick and Zeb had located him—and so had Natalie. And if it hadn't been her…

Someone else would have come for him. It was clear now—his parentage had been a ticking time bomb. He was still trying to get his head around it.

And failing. He looked at his Christmas tree—the one he had gone out and cut for Natalie. He hadn't plugged in the lights and the whole thing looked sad and forlorn. Tomorrow, he'd take off all the decorations and carefully pack them away in the bins. Then he would take the tree outside and burn it.

And that would be the end of him and Natalie Baker.

* * *

"And stay tuned for *A Good Morning*, where ther
will be some shocking new revelations about th
Beaumont family," the morning news lady said wit
a smile at the camera.

CJ groaned. He was torturing himself by watchin
Natalie's station. Yes, part of it was self-preservatior
He needed to know what was being said about him
Was his sex life about to become common knowledge
Had she taken more pictures of him or of his house
Would she display the star he'd given her like a hun
ing trophy? Would his friends and neighbors show
up on TV, talking about how they never would've
guessed there was a Beaumont lurking in their midst

Forewarned was forearmed. But it was also th
highest form of masochism he could imagine.

It had been six days since he had literally dragge
Natalie off of his property. Six long days that ha
been filled with a barrage of emails and phone calls
After he'd gotten her back to the county road, th
temperatures had dropped and everything had ice
over so, at the very least, he hadn't had visitors. Th
roads were still too tricky for a bunch of city slick
ers to make it out this far. But that would chang
soon, he knew.

God, look at that—he had his own damn graphic
now. The Missing Beaumont Bastard flashed in gray
and red—the brewery colors.

Jesus. This was beyond him, which really only

eft him one option. He picked up his phone and di-
led Daniel Lee.

"I take it you saw the teaser?" Daniel said without any other introduction.

It didn't matter what time CJ called, Daniel always answered on the first ring and always seemed
o be watching the exact same thing.

"It's never going to end, is it?" Natalie had enough
on him to stretch this out for months if she wanted to.

True, she hadn't exactly been forthcoming with
he information on all the episodes he'd watched so
far. But it was only a matter of time.

"It will, eventually," Daniel added. "You've only
been in the public eye for less than a week. It's
New Year's Eve—I guarantee that tonight, someone, somewhere will do something more interesting than you."

"You think?"

"I know. Personally? I've never met a man as boring as you are."

CJ had to laugh at that. "Thanks, I think."

"It's a good thing," Daniel reassured him. "You're
not just the most boring Beaumont, you're boring,
period. There's not a single exciting thing about you
and the public craves excitement. You'll see. Another
week or two and who knows."

CJ desperately wanted to believe that—but he
couldn't. Natalie knew him too well. He was tired
of waiting for the other shoe to drop. "You really

think I should go public?" That was what Danie
had been arguing for the last week—if they trotte
CJ out and demonstrated to the world exactly hov
boring he was, people would lose interest faster. Th
mystery would be gone and without that, there wa
nothing to tease.

"Absolutely. Why? You change your mind?"

"Yeah." It felt like a defeat—but he had beei
beaten the moment Natalie Baker and walked into th
Firestone Grain and Feed. "What are the options?"

There was a pause. "There are three viable options—
although I'm open to suggestions. First, we hold a pres
conference."

"Like Zeb did on the steps of the Beaumont Brew
ery? No." He had absolutely no desire to parade him
self before a pack of bloodthirsty reporters and wai
for the body blows.

Daniel chuckled. "I didn't say it was the best idea
You can also come into town tonight and put in ar
appearance at a New Year's Eve party. I can think
of three venues that would provide an appropriate
amount of press coverage without leaving you exposed."

CJ scowled at the phone. "That doesn't seem like
my style." Better than a press conference, but not by
much. "What's the third option?"

"The Beaumont family is going to be hosting ar
Epiphany party—that's January sixth." CJ rolled
his eyes. He knew when Epiphany was. "It will be

mostly family along with close friends. We could invite one or two reporters, give them exclusive access. I would expect you to do a short interview and smile for a few pictures. The angle would be that we were all one big happy family, of course."

"I wouldn't be the focus?" Because he had no interest in being the center of a news story where the Beaumont family welcomed their long-lost half brothers into the fold.

"I believe there would be some other announcements at this party as well. So I don't believe you would be the focus for long."

CJ thought about it. Assuming the roads were clear, he could do that. Finally, after all these years, he wouldn't run away from the idea of being a Beaumont. Instead, he was going to walk toward them. And hopefully be immediately overshadowed by some "other announcements." "All right."

There was another long pause before Daniel said, "Any idea what the shocking new revelation is going to be in ten minutes?"

CJ tried very hard not to groan out loud. His idea of hell was having his sex life discussed on TV. "No idea," he lied. But even as he did, he felt the muscle in his jaw twitch. And that made him think of Natalie all over again. Even his own mother had never figured out he had a tell. Natalie had *seen* him more than anyone else ever had. "Have you been able to contact her?"

That was one of the things Daniel was doing—talking to the media people and trying to, as Natalie had put it, *redirect* the attention. And Natalie was a media person.

"She's not taking my calls." That couldn't be good. "I tell you what, though—she's a hell of an investigative reporter."

"Yeah? Well, I guess so—she found me, after all." Although that wasn't quite as hard as CJ had once thought it would be, apparently.

"She didn't just find *you*," Daniel said. "She didn't start with you. She was digging in to me long before she tracked you down."

CJ frowned. She hadn't said anything about that to him. But then, she hadn't told him everything, had she? "Yeah? Did she find anything on you?"

"No. I've got too many firewalls. But she got close and she tripped some of my early warning systems." He whistled in low appreciation.

"What—are you in to her?"

His brother just chuckled. "No. Blondes aren't my type. But there's a lot of political wisdom in keeping your friends close and your enemies closer. I'd hire her if I could. Her brains plus her looks—and her dedication? She could rob banks and get away with it scot-free."

CJ started to laugh.

"What?"

"I told her the same thing. I don't think she would

take a job working for you, though. That show's the most important thing in the world to her." More important than he had been.

"Well, if you talk to her again, tell her I pay well." There was an ominous undertone to that statement, and CJ was reminded again that he did not know very much about Daniel. But then again, apparently neither did anyone else—what with all the firewalls and safety features and stuff.

He was probably overthinking it. Daniel was also the executive vice president at the Beaumont Brewery now. Having someone as high-profile as Natalie work for him would probably be a coup or something.

"Yeah, I don't think we're going to see each other again. But," he added, "if I do, I'll mention it."

"Thanks," Daniel said. "I'll get you the invitation to the party."

They ended the call just as the morning news anchor cut over to Natalie's show. The theme music and graphics played out over the screen and there she was, smiling at the camera just like she did every day. If CJ hadn't spent so much time with her, he wouldn't have noticed any difference—but now, he could.

Even though she was smiling and perky, her eyes had a dead look to them. Was that how she'd always looked on television? He was pretty sure—but it wasn't who she was. Because now he knew what she looked like when she was happy or upset or—

God help him—aroused. He hated that he could tell the difference, but more than that, he hated that he cared. It wasn't his fault she had that look in her eyes. She had brought this upon both of them.

He didn't want to hear what she had to say but he couldn't look away.

"Good morning, Denver." She batted her eyelashes at the camera like she did every day, but something seemed off. She looked tense. Oh, God—was this it? Was his sex life about to become a lead story?

"This is going to be my last morning with you here on *A Good Morning*. I've decided to step away from television. Recently, I compromised not only my journalistic credibility, but also my personal code of honor. I took a picture of someone I care for and uploaded it to the internet without his permission. Here at *A Good Morning*, we pride ourselves on a higher standard of behavior. I wanted to take this time to thank each and every one of you for tuning in and for following me on social media. I'm going to be pulling back my online presence as well, but when I'm ready for something new—" she swallowed "—I will be sure and let my fans know."

"Liar," he muttered at the TV. She was seriously doing this? Was she seriously quitting live on the air? Because…of what? Because of *him*?

His heart began to pound wildly in his chest. She was. He was afraid that he might be hallucinating this—it was all wishful thinking after his conversation with Daniel. But then she looked at the camera and said, "To CJ Wesley and the people of Firestone, I apologize. I confused 'likes' and 'shares' with hope and happiness. My mistake was valuing comments and reach more than I did family and friends. So, as the station moves forward into the New Year, this program will be moving forward with the new host, a man you'll all enjoy spending time with, Kevin Durante and—" he saw her swallow again "—I think you're going to like it. Starting January first—tomorrow—I hope you tune in for *A Great Morning with Kevin Durante*. Thank you for making me a part of your lives for the last seven years. And I hope each and every one of you have a happy New Year."

The show cut to commercial, but CJ barely noticed. That was *it*? That was the shocking announcement? Not a discussion of his prowess in bed or interviews with his old girlfriends?

Natalie had quit. Because of him. He hadn't asked her to—he was sure about that.

His cell phone lit up. Good or bad? Daniel texted.

Good, I think, he texted back.

You sure you're not going to see her anymore?

I have no idea, CJ replied honestly. But he was thinking that maybe…

He just might be seeing her sooner than he had planned.

Like now. Like right *now*. He could get his truck

and, assuming he didn't skate into a ditch in the next fifteen miles, be in Denver within an hour. He ought to be able to find directions to the studio online, right? It would take her at least that long to get off the air and pack up her desk, right?

If you do, my offer of a job for her stands. Put a good word in for me.

CJ didn't even bother to reply. He was already up and shoving his arms into his sheepskin coat. Keys. He needed the truck's keys. And dammit, it was supposed to start snowing anytime—but he didn't care. He had to get to downtown Denver *now*.

He threw open the front door and hit the porch at a dead run—only to come to a skidding halt. For there, coming down the driveway, was a red Mustang.

Thirteen

Natalie felt so weird right now. Seeing this place again—it was almost too much. It'd only been a week since she'd left but it felt like a lifetime ago.

She had no idea if she was doing the right thing. Part of her was nearly paralyzed with fear. She had quit. And by now, the show had aired and there would be no going back. No doubt people were going to rake her over the coals. Only this time, she wouldn't be there to watch it unfold in real time.

But the other part? She rounded the bend and CJ's house came into view. The rest of her was anything but panicked. She didn't care what anyone thought. She really only cared what one person thought—CJ. She had hurt him and she was hoping that she could make it right—but she didn't know if that was possible. Still, knowing that she was here for him, instead of for ratings or reach, was freeing.

As she got closer to the house, she saw the front door fly open and CJ come running out. He looked half-crazed and for a second, she considered putting the car in Reverse and bailing. This was not a good idea in a long string of bad ideas. She shouldn't have come. She was crazy to think that he might accept her apology. She was crazy to think that he might want her back.

But if that made her nuts, so be it.

When he saw her, he came to a screeching halt and just stared as she got out of the car. For a long moment, neither of them said anything. Which, in the grand scheme of things, was probably progress. At the very least, he wasn't telling her to go to hell, so that had to count for something, right?

"You're here," he said in a strangled voice. "I thought you were at the studio—your show?"

"We taped it two days ago." She'd spent the last two days wondering if she should go back and unresign. If the segment hadn't aired, had she really quit?

But Steve wouldn't have taken her back, anyway. Kevin had a shiny new show and Steve was happy for a chance to take another crack at the ratings and...

And they wouldn't miss her. But that wasn't the important thing, she'd discovered.

No, the more important thing was that *she* wouldn't miss *them*. What a revelation that had been—and she never would have had it without the man before her.

She had missed CJ. All she could do was hope that he had missed her, too. "I, um, I brought you a Christmas present." She took a deep breath and braced for the worst. If he were going to tell her to get the hell off of his property, now would probably be when it happened.

"It's not Christmas anymore," he said, staring at her as if she were a ghost.

"I know." She pulled her phone out of her pocket and held it out for him. "Here."

He looked down at the red bow she tied around the middle of it. But the bow wasn't big enough to hide the shattered screen. "What the hell happened to your phone?"

It was important to keep breathing. It would be silly if she passed out now. "I took a hatchet to it. After I deleted all my social media accounts. Aside from a few photos, there wasn't anything on there that I wanted to keep."

"I didn't ask you to delete your accounts. You didn't have to do that for me."

"I didn't." She took a deep breath. "I needed to do it for me. I might go back online, but it'll be on my terms this time. I need to... I don't know. I need to keep the negative out and that was so wrapped up with who I was that I just had to burn it down and start over."

His mouth was open and he was staring at her, and then her phone, and then back at her. It was a hard thing to watch, so she dropped her gaze. "What about your phone numbers? Your contacts?"

She shrugged. "I quit. My job, that is."

He took a step toward her. "So I saw. I saw your apology, too."

"I meant it. I made a mistake, CJ. I let a moment of panic overrule my judgment. I should've had faith in you. Because you're real. You are a real, honest, decent man and… And I don't know very many people like you. So I didn't know how to act around you."

When he didn't say anything, she looked up at him. He managed to get his mouth closed, but his head was tilted to the side and he stared at her in open confusion. "I just did what anyone would do."

"No, you didn't—don't you see? I've never known *anyone* like you. You don't know how special you are and…" She squeezed her eyes shut so that she wouldn't do anything ridiculous, like start crying. "And I let you down. I ruined everything."

His face hardened. "Who said that to you?"

"What?"

"Who told you that you ruined everything?"

She blushed from the tips of her ears to her toes. This was one of her most painful memories. "My mom." If he had been anyone else in the world, she vouldn't have told him. But he had asked for honsty and she had absolutely nothing left to give him xcept the truth. "I was six, I think, and I didn't get vhat I wanted from Santa so I threw a fit and she told ne that I was a spoiled brat and I ruined everything and I always had and I always would. Her body, her narriage, her career—*Christmas*. I ruined Christmas." She wrapped her arms around her waist, trying to ease the tightness there. "And then she left. She left and I've never seen her again."

His mouth flopped open again. No, he didn't know how special he was—how lucky he was to have two parents who loved him and protected him. "And your dad?"

She shrugged. "I ruined Christmas. So we stopped having one. I don't think he ever forgave me or her." She straightened up, turned on a brave face. "I did not save his phone number to my new phone. Every year I try to call him and every year, it hurts more. I'm going to stop trying to please other people. It doesn't matter."

"It does," he told her. "You were six—that matters." He took another step closer to her—close enough now that she could feel the warmth from his body. "And you don't ruin everything, Natalie. I don't ever want to hear you say that again."

She closed her eyes again. "I ruined *us*. You gave me my phone back and I immediately took a photo. I didn't plan on uploading it. I didn't. I just wanted something to remind me of the best week of my life when it ended. And then my dad told me I'd ruined his Christmas again and told me to leave him alone and…and I panicked. I had this moment where I felt like I was nothing all over again and I was going to lose my show and without that, who am I?"

"Natalie…"

She shook her head. "I'm not telling you this to make you feel sorry for me. I just want you to understand that I was trying to find a compromise between what you wanted and what I thought I wanted and a semi-random Santa photo seemed the safest way to make our two worlds meet. But I was wrong about that. And I'm sorry."

The next thing she knew, she was folded into his arms. She didn't want to hug him back—she didn't want him to think that she needed this. Even if she did, just a little.

"My mom lives in fear of the Beaumonts," he said softly. "I always knew that Hardwick was my birth father because she told me that he might come for me one day and that if anyone named Beaumont ever showed up, I should run the other way or hide or scream. Beaumonts were dangerous and I had to be protected from them."

She leaned back in his arms and looked at him. "Really? I mean, I guess that makes sense—he usually kept the children in the divorces. But he was never married to your mother."

"Trust me, I know."

She was having trouble thinking with his arms round her, so she stepped away from him. "And Hardwick is dead, anyway."

For the first time, he smiled. "I knew that—but I don't think I understood it. Does that make sense? It was so ingrained in me to be afraid of the Beaumonts that, even after he was dead, I didn't stop hiding. But they're just people." He reached up and brushed a strand of hair away from her cheek. "I'm going to go to an Epiphany party with them on the sixth. I'll talk to a couple of reporters and be as boring as possible and then wait for the story to die."

She gasped at him. "You'll *what*?"

He shot her a crooked grin. "It's still going to upset my mother. She made a good life for herself and for me and she doesn't want anyone to think about a mistake that she might have made a long time ago. But I don't have to hide. I don't have to be afraid of who I might be." He stared down at her. "We all make mistakes, Natalie. It's how we make up for them that counts."

This time, she was the one who hugged him. "I—I don't know if I should apologize for finding you or not. If I hadn't, nothing would've changed. I would still be doing a job that made me sick, and you…"

"And I would be alone," he said into her hair.

She didn't know how long they stood there like that, but finally, the cold began to catch up with her.

She had dressed better today—her own jeans and boots and a chunky turtleneck sweater. But they were still standing outside and the temperature was dropping. So, even though she didn't want to, she pulled herself out of his arms. "So."

His grin got slightly less crooked. "So," he agreed.

She hadn't realized she was still holding her dead phone until he plucked it from her hands. He looked down at it as if he couldn't believe she had really smashed the damn thing, and then he reared back and threw it. "What are you going to do now?"

"Honestly? I'm not sure. I'm unemployed and I think I'm going to sell my condo. It's Natalie Baker's condo—and I don't feel like that person anymore. But I don't know how to do anything else. My whole life has been one long con game of trying to convince people I'm something that I'm not and now that I'm not going to do that anymore…" She shrugged. "I'm at a loss." His eyebrows jumped up and he looked like he was going to say something—so she hurried to cut him off. "I didn't come out here to ask if I could stay. I just wanted to apologize, CJ."

He mulled this over. "Apology accepted. And I wanted to say that I'm sorry, too."

Now was her turn to stare at him. "What? *Why?* You didn't do anything wrong. I was the one at fault."

"I don't think it's such a bad thing, being a Beaumont. Suddenly, I've gone from being an only child to having all these brothers and sisters who want to

eet me. I'm not going to pretend I'm going to like
ll of them, but…" He shrugged. "It was always this
rrible thing in my mind and I don't think it is so ter-
ble in reality. So when I found out that you'd taken
hat picture, I was still acting like you had ruined my
fe. And I'm not proud of how I treated you. But I
on't think you ruined anything."

Unexpectedly, her throat closed up. It was sweet
f him to say that, but they both knew the truth.
I'm glad to hear that." She may not have ruined his
fe, but she didn't think there was any hope for the
wo of them.

She should leave, she decided, and as she turned
way a snowflake landed on her cheek. She looked
p at the sky. It wasn't a rolling wall of clouds bar-
eling down on her—but it was beginning to snow.

"Where are you going?" CJ asked, stepping to the
ide and blocking her path back to her car.

"I should leave before the weather gets really
ad."

"Don't."

"What?"

He stared at her, his jaw tightening. "Don't leave.
 want you to stay. It's New Year's Eve." He took a
leep breath and then reached out a hand toward her.
I want you to stay with me."

"CJ, you can't be serious." Could he? Now that she
hought about it, had he ever *not* been serious? He did
what he said and he said what he did. There were no

games when it came to CJ Wesley. "I screwed up! I took that picture of you and I posted it, remember?"

He looked off in the distance, where, maybe twenty or thirty feet away, her phone had met its final end. "Yeah, okay—you did. But I'm not going to think about what you did anymore. Instead, I'm going to think about what you didn't do. You didn't run back to Denver and broadcast all of my secrets. You didn't kiss and tell. Hell, except for that one photo, you didn't even say anything about my town."

"But that's not the end of it. Other people are talking, and other reporters will keep digging—and that's my fault."

He shrugged as if this were seriously no big deal. "This, too, shall pass. It's not just me against the Beaumonts. It's the Beaumonts against the world. I've got a family who's going to stand beside me and that's something I only have because of you, Natalie." He grinned and brushed another snowflake of her cheek. "Besides, I have a job for you."

She looked at him hard, trying to ignore the way his touch warmed her skin. "A job? Are you serious?"

"You talk about yourself as if you're useless—a talking head. But that's not what I see. I see someone who's intelligent and beautiful and whose capacity for kindness is there." She rolled her eyes, and he added, "It hasn't been nurtured properly, but it's there. And you did something that very few people have done—you found me."

"But that doesn't mean I'm qualified for a ranch job." Because if he were asking her to stay...

Well, it would be tempting. When they had been snowed in, she had wanted nothing more than for that time to never end.

But she wasn't a ranch wife. She didn't really cook. The only thing she had that would recommend her to that position was the fact that she was used to getting up early, but that wasn't enough.

"You're a little too shy around horses to be a good ranch hand," he said with a chuckle. "No, Daniel Lee has offered to hire you. He knows exactly how far you got trying to dig up information on him and he was impressed. And according to him, you're brilliant—and more tenacious than a private eye. Plus, you know how to handle the media. If you're interested, I could call him right now."

Her mouth dropped open as she stared at him. "You're lying." But even as she said it, she knew he wasn't. Not a single muscle in his jaw had twitched.

"Hand to God," he said, grinning wildly.

More snow fell from the sky. They were working their way close to full-on flurries. His hair was turning white and his beard was catching flakes. Soon the roads would get slick and her Mustang was not any better equipped for that than it had been two weeks ago.

"You know what else I'm not lying about?" he asked, stepping into her again and dusting snow off of her shoulders. "I'm not lying when I say that I want you to stay. You made me feel like it was okay that I was a Beaumont *and* a Wesley. You knew my deepest secret—but for the most part, it didn't matter."

"But it did, don't you see? I ruined—"

"No, you didn't. You *changed* things, Natalie— things that, in retrospect, needed to be changed." He leaned down and touched his forehead to hers. "You changed me for the better."

"How can you say that?" Because it didn't make any sense. She had hurt him—she knew she had. And anyone else would have held that against her. Including her own parents. Especially her own parents.

"Because it's the truth, babe. I accept your apology. I forgive you. And I hope you can forgive me for overreacting."

She couldn't stop the tears this time. Forgiveness? She'd come out here with the intent to apologize— and that was it. Forgiveness was such a foreign concept to her it hadn't even occurred to her as an option.

But she saw that he was right. She'd only been a little girl when she threw a temper tantrum. Probably every kid did that at some point—even him. It wasn't her fault that her mother had walked out. Her parents were messed up if they couldn't even forgive a little kid for doing something that all little kids did.

"Of course I do," she said, her voice trembling.

he wrapped her arms around his waist and held
m tight. "I'm not any good at this. I'm trying so
ard, CJ. But I'm going to screw things up. Things
at you think anyone would do? It's all new to me.
ut I want…"

She wanted it all and, no matter what he said, she
wasn't sure she deserved it.

He tilted her head back and looked her in the eyes.
He was only a breath away. "Just be honest, Natalie.
The truth—that's all I've ever wanted from you."

"You changed me, too. You made me realize that
could be worth something to someone. You made
me want to be good enough for you."

"You are. You're good for me. And I want you to
stay. Stay for the New Year." His lips brushed against
her, damp from the snow. "Stay forever."

She jolted in his arms. *"What?"*

"I love you," he said, and damn if he didn't sound
completely serious. "Let's get married, Natalie."

She cupped his face in her hands. "You want to
marry *me*?"

"I do. I trust my gut." Not a single muscle in his
face moved—except for that smile. Oh, that grin of
his warmed her heart—and a few other places. "And
you? Is that what you want?"

"Yes," she whispered.

Just then, the snow began to fall in earnest. CJ
swept her up and spun her around, kissing her like
she was worth something. She *was*. It would take

some work, but this was New Year's Eve—a time for starting over, a time for hope. And, maybe for the first time, she dared to hope.

CJ looked up at the sky. "We might be snowed in for a little bit..."

"After last time, I resolved that I wouldn't go any where without a week's worth of clothes in the car."

CJ laughed and Natalie laughed with him. "Come on," he said, opening the door to her car so she could snag the duffel bag. "Let's ring in the New Year properly."

"Promise me," she said, leaning into him as they walked up to the house, "that we will always celebrate Christmas."

He turned and pulled her into a fierce kiss. "Always," he whispered against her lips.

For the rest of their lives, they would keep Christmas in their hearts.

* * * * *

COMING NEXT MONTH FROM

HARLEQUIN™ *Desire*

Available January 3, 2017

HDCNM12

SPECIAL EXCERPT FROM

HARLEQUIN® *Desire*

en CEO Wesley Jackson's Twitter account is hacked,
it's to reveal that he has a secret daughter! Amid
ndal, he tracks down his old fling, but can he convince
er he's truly ready to be a father—and a husband?

Read on for a sneak peek at
THE TYCOON'S SECRET CHILD
y USA TODAY *bestselling author Maureen Child,*
the first story in the new
XAS CATTLEMAN'S CLUB: BLACKMAIL *series!*

ook where your dallying has gotten you," the email
d.

"What the hell?" There was an attachment, and even
ugh Wes had a bad feeling about all of this, he opened
The photograph popped onto his computer screen.

Staring down at the screen, his gaze locked on the
age of the little girl staring back at him. "What the—"

She looked just like him.

Panic and fury tangled up inside him and tightened
to a knot that made him feel like he was choking.

A daughter? He had a child. Judging by the picture,
e looked to be four or five years old, so unless it was
old photo, there was only one woman who could be
e girl's mother. And just like that, the woman was back,
ont and center in his mind.

How the hell had this happened? Stupid. He knew how
had happened. What he didn't know was why he hadn't

been told. Wes rubbed one hand along the back o
neck. Still staring at the smiling girl on the screer
opened a new window and went to Twitter.

Somebody had hacked his account. His new acc
name was, as promised in the email, Deadbeatdad.
didn't get this stopped fast, it would go viral and m
start interfering with his business.

Instantly, Wes made some calls and turned the n
over to his IT guys to figure out. Meanwhile, he
too late to stop #Deadbeatdad from spreading.
Twitterverse was already moving on it. Now he
a child to find and a reputation to repair. Snatching
the phone, he stabbed the button for his assistant's de
"Robin," he snapped. "Get Mike from PR in here now

He didn't even wait to hear her response, just slamm
the phone down and went back to his computer.
brought up the image of the little girl—his daughte
again and stared at her. What was her name? Where
she live?

Then thoughts of the woman who had to be t
girl's mother settled into his brain. Isabelle Gray. Sh
disappeared from his life years ago—apparently with
child.

Jaw tight, eyes narrowed, Wes promised himself
was going to get to the bottom of all of this.

Don't miss
THE TYCOON'S SECRET CHILD
by USA TODAY *bestselling author Maureen Child,*
available now wherever
Harlequin® Desire *books and ebooks are sold.*

www.Harlequin.com

Whatever You're Into… Passionate Reads

Looking for more passionate reads from Harlequin®? Fear not! Harlequin® Presents, Harlequin® Desire and Harlequin® Blaze offer you irresistible romance stories featuring powerful heroes.

♦HARLEQUIN® *Presents*

Do you want alpha males, decadent glamour and jet-set lifestyles? Step into the sensational, sophisticated world of Harlequin® Presents, where sinfully tempting heroes ignite a fierce and wickedly irresistible passion!

♦HARLEQUIN® *Desire*

Harlequin® Desire novels are powerful, passionate and provocative contemporary romances set against a backdrop of wealth, privilege and sweeping family saga. Alpha heroes with a soft side meet strong-willed but vulnerable heroines amid a dramatic world of divided loyalties, high-stakes conflict and intense emotion.

♦HARLEQUIN® *Blaze*

Harlequin® Blaze stories sizzle with strong heroines and irresistible heroes playing the game of modern love and lust. They're fun, sexy and always steamy.

Be sure to check out our full selection of books within each series every month!

www.Harlequin.com

HPASSION2016